HEART'S LOCK, LOVE'S KEY

A VALENTINE'S DAY ANTHOLOGY

ROCHELLE WOLF   AMELIA S. FLETCHER

MAGGIE FRANCIS   HEATHER GREY   MARRON KAYE

MADELINE NIXON   LAURA MEREDITH   ALYSSA MILANI

BECKY TZAG   L.E. WAGENSVELD

CONTENTS

INTRODUCTION

Welcome to Heart's Lock, Love's Key!

Whether you read it all in one sitting or savour it like the best chocolate, we are thrilled to share this collection of love-themed stories in honour of Valentine's Day. Each scintillating tale was created especially for this anthology, and the moments of joy within range from sweet to spicy.

If one or all of these talented Canadian authors resonates with you, we hope you'll spread the word and share the love!

AND THEY SAY ROMANCE IS DEAD

ALYSSA MILANI

Tropes:

- Contemporary romance
- Instant attraction
- Strangers to lovers

Content Warnings: explicit sex scene, brief mention of grief.

Author's Note: This story is the spin-off of the novel *As Far As We Knew*.

GROWING UP POOR, we never truly got to celebrate the holidays. There were no presents under the Christmas tree or eggs for easter. And there most certainly wasn't chocolate or roses for Valentine's Day. I always dreamed about being pampered on this special day but was never given the chance. Truthfully, people spend hundreds, thousands even, for a single day to spoil their partner. When every other day of the year is just forgotten.

What's so special about *this* day?

Okay, maybe I'm a little sour because I've never celebrated Valentine's Day. I've never been in a relationship long enough to merit being spoiled—truthfully, I've never *been* spoiled. So as time went on, I've become that heathen that loathes all holidays and all the consumer bullshit it comes with.

Yet here I am wearing a pastel pink strapless dress, standing in the corner of my best friend's apartment on Valentine's Day while we celebrate her recent engagement.

The apartment is cream-coloured with couches and furniture to match the traditional décor. The white kitchen has all the food and alcohol on the large marble island. I spent the better part of my day helping set up the engagement party with signs, and tassels, and blowing up balloons. It's pink-themed, too, which adds to the cheesiness of this day.

I've lost count of how many drinks I've had or how many eye rolls I've given. But I try to be appropriate because tonight is about her, no matter how much this day blows. I have to mask my feelings with smiles and congratulations because I'm the maid of honour.

Sipping my drink, my eye darts to the front door as it opens to a tall brunet stepping into the apartment with black ink running up and down his arms. The tight pink polo hugs his taut muscles, beige slacks leave no imagination to the size of his...thighs. But when I catch the mismatched Converse he has on, a snort escapes me, immediately catching his attention.

His smile brightens, eyes drinking me in, but he doesn't come to me. Not yet anyway. He does his rounds of the apartment, hugging people, laughing, and talking. There's a familiarity about his energy, a want building within me that hasn't been tamed in a while. This is my best friend's night, but it's also Valentine's Day. The night of love *and* lust.

Not once does the brunet grace me with a delicious smile. But he does make sure to keep his back to me most of the evening throwing me with his "hard to get" attitude when I know for a fact he can sense my eyes on him. It's in his movements; the way he flexes his bicep when he does a shot, the way he laughs a little louder than needed. A charmer at work.

Brushing my wavy blonde hair off my shoulder, I drain the rest of my drink and sigh. One of two things will happen tonight. I'll drink myself stupid and have to sleep in the guest room...or I'll still drink myself stupid but make a fool of myself and ruin this evening.

To avoid my best friend being mad at me, I don't go to the kitchen for a refill and instead fold my arm across my stomach, holding the empty cup at my lips.

Music thumps in the kitchen causing me to bring my attention to it. The friends my best friend made over the years crowd around her, *oohing* and *awwing* at her diamond ring that costs more than two months' rent. I should be over there with them, but I know myself. I'll start badmouthing how expensive the ring is and how that money could have been put to good use.

But I let her have her moment, after all, she deserves it.

The brunet in the pink polo slides over to me, making me chuckle as he dances with his upper body, shaking his shoulders and moving his arms in front of him.

"Hey," he says, sticking his tongue between his teeth.

I raise my empty cup to him. "Hey yourself."

"What're you doing here all by yourself instead of joining the party?" He's still dancing slightly, moving his feet to the beat.

Tilting my head from side to side, I sigh softly. "I don't know anyone here aside from Kaylee—the bride-to-be."

"Then mingle."

Laughing, I continue to curl the cup to my chest and raise my eyebrows as he dances around me. "Easy for you to say. The thought of small talk gives me this stabbing pain right here." I tap my forehead. "I hate people."

"Hate's a strong word."

"Dislike." Narrowing my eyes, I shrug. "Okay, maybe not 'dislike' as much as 'uncomfortable with crowds'. They give me the ick."

He chuckles, nodding softly. "If it makes you feel any better, I did four shots before I arrived to help ease the awkwardness of this day."

"The engagement party?"

He grimaces. "No."

"Valentine's Day?"

Flashing me with finger guns. "Bullshit holiday if you ask me."

Heat radiates from my cheeks as my heart blooms in satisfaction. He knows the way to my heart. "Please, do go on."

He laughs, stuffing his hands in his pockets. "Every relationship I've ever been in, they seem to always break up with me on Valentine's Day. Y'know, after I buy them flowers and gifts and take them to dinner. Then bam, *sorry, it's not you, it's me.* Or *maybe we should start seeing other people.* And the last one—definitely my favorite—*you shower too much.*"

"What?" A boisterous laugh leaves me, causing a couple of people to glance over. "How many times a day do you shower?"

"Once."

Scrunching my chin. "That's a normal amount, right? What's a normal shower routine?" Gasping sarcastically, I put my hand on my mouth. "Have I been showering wrong all this time?"

He can't contain his laughter, looking out at the crowd before returning his green eyes to me. "She legit told me she prefers me ripe, who says that?"

I'm laughing to tears now, wiping the makeup that's probably smeared from under my eyes. "Hey, don't shame people for their kinks."

Licking his lips, his eyes trail to mine, holding steadily. His smile doesn't fade when I rake my teeth on my bottom lip. "What's your story, then? Why are you alone on this Valentine's Day?"

Raising my brow, I bring the cup to my lips and groan at the fact that it's empty, I had forgotten. "Who says I'm alone?"

"You just told me you don't know anyone here."

"And who says my partner isn't in the bathroom or running late or something?"

He lifts a shoulder, seeing right through my lies. "Well, if your partner is running late, shame on them. You're not someone who should wait on anyone."

I try to ignore the double beat my heart does, but it's hard not to ignore when he dips his head down, moving closer to me and smelling of cinnamon and sandalwood.

Inhaling softly, I attempt to compose myself even though my legs feel like jelly. "What about you? Which one of these women broke up with you tonight?"

He chuckles, taking a step back yet remaining close enough so that the scent lingers a moment longer. "It's been three years since someone broke up with me. This day has become the one day I spoil myself with an expensive bottle of whisky and an extra-large pizza."

Waggling my eyebrows, we break eye contact and look off at the crowd. "And yet, here we both are wallowing in how much this holiday blows."

"I was told not to ruin this evening. Greg, the groom-to-be, lent me this outfit." He scoffs, pinching some of the fabric of the polo and tugging it away from his body. "Who owns something this *pink*?"

"That explains the shoes."

He laughs, rolling onto the balls of his feet and then back to the tip of his toes, looking down at his Converse. The left foot is black canvas, and the right one is red. "Yep, had to rebel against the machine somehow."

"Those goddamn machines." I shake a fist in the air, getting another laugh out of him that crinkles the skin around his eyes. It's a deep, savoury laugh. The kind that makes you smile even on your darkest days. "But I'll have you know a lot of people own pink. This was hanging in my closet."

He takes my hand, igniting a spark that shoots our gazes together and spins me. "This is one helluva dress." His voice is low, husky, and breathy. Like he can feel the pulsating tingle coursing through my veins with his warm hand in mine.

"I only pull out the good stuff for crappy holidays."

He doesn't let go of my hand, but lowers it and slowly twines our fingers. It feels right, it always has. "Yeah? What other holidays do you hate?"

"Christmas."

"You're a monster! Who hates Christmas?" He's facing me, our chests inches apart. I can practically taste the liquor on his breath—cinnamon from the Fireball whisky in the kitchen.

Lifting a shoulder in a shy shrug, I look into my empty drink and sigh. "We didn't have a lot of money growing up so when Christmas rolled around, I was lucky to get socks as a kid." The pity in his gaze makes my cheeks darken and my eyes glass over, but I blink the tears away when I glance at my best friend having the time of her life. "Until I met Kaylee, my life was complete trash. She made Christmas that much better, but I still dislike it out of nostalgia. I'm hipster like that."

He straightens out his shoulders, smiling down at me. "I'll make you fall in love with Christmas again. It'll be my goal this year to make—"

"Sutton."

"—Sutton, fall in love with Christmas...among other things," he finishes with a wink.

His thumb brushes along mine, and not a hint of uncomfortableness spreads through me as we hold hands like it's just the two of us here, not an entire apartment filled with people.

"Define other things...?" I thin my eyes, waiting for him to give me his name.

"Lockland."

Nodding, his eyes trace the outline of my face as my cheeks bloom a deep crimson before his eyes trail to my neck and settle on a necklace I haven't taken off since I was a child. "Keys?" His other hand comes up and touches the necklace, letting the tips of his fingers brush against my chest before he drops his hand.

My hand slips from his and I touch the necklace. Three small keys about half an inch in length hang off a gold chain. "My grandmother gave this to me before she died. Told me whenever I was feeling low, I could use a key to open a door to new adventures that would brighten my spirits."

His gaze is fixated on the keys, watching as I play with them between my fingers. "Have you ever used any?"

An exasperated laugh pools from my lips in a quick burst. "If these keys disappeared whenever I used them, they would've been gone within a week."

As he reaches out to touch them again, cheers and claps summon our attention. Lockland and I stare at each other before a shy grin spreads to his lips and he scratches the shadow of a beard on his face.

The crowd in the kitchen silences as Kaylee and Greg clink their glasses. "We want to thank everyone for coming and celebrating this moment with us. Finding love at such a young age is so rare yet important. And I can't thank the stars enough for giving me this beautiful gem," Kaylee says, leaning forward to kiss her fiancé.

She giggles afterward, hugging him as she turns to everyone. "Okay, okay. I saw this on TikTok. It's a cute and fun token from our closest friends and family to add to our wedding video. I want to go around and hear everyone's impression of—"

"Wanna get out of here?" I ask Lockland, our fingers grazing at our sides. "There's no way in hell I'm sharing anything on video."

He drags a hand down his face. "I'm the best man."

"And I'm the maid of honour."

My best friend has always been the romantic type. She had a wedding binder under her bed from the age of nine. Getting married at twenty-four is not something too shocking for any of us. Greg's good for her and makes her happy; that's all I can ask for.

Lockland smirks, nodding. "I live three floors down."

"Booze?"

"Of course, is that even a question?"

Taking my purse from the couch behind me, I jerk my head at the door. "Let's go, then."

He smiles, threads his fingers through mine, and tiptoes like a cartoon character toward the door. I can't help but laugh at his childlike attitude. He's much like me in a way, sees the world as something amusing rather than taking everything seriously. Probably why I live with four roommates, can't hold down a job, and haven't been in a relationship that lasted longer than four months.

He jogs down the stairs, letting go of my hand when I can't keep up, but how could I in these five-inch stilettos? They seemed like a good idea at the time. Now, I'm cursing whoever invented high heels.

Lockland stops at the bottom of the stairs, looking up at me as I descend as quickly as I can. Even in the way his eyes explore, eating up every inch of exposed flesh, I feel the most beautiful I've ever felt.

"God, you're sexy."

A snorted laugh escapes me, taking in his smirk. "Oh, don't let this tipsy walk fool you, I'm a mess."

Without question, he steps forward, hands on my hips, and lifts me the rest of the way down the stairs, holding my body close to his.

Our hearts beat as one, rhythmic and unsteady. Just like our breaths.

The corner of his lip tugs as he pulls it in and bites down. "I could kiss you right now and I don't even know you."

"Sutton, best friend of the bride. Kind of hilarious, mainly anxious. Hates people and Christmas, mainly Valentine's Day. I love red licorice, cherry soda, and chocolate ice cream—they're basically my three food groups. Birthday is in May and—"

He slams his lips on mine, adjusting my legs around his waist. His lips are soft, demanding. Massaging mine with angst like it's something he's been dying to do for years.

I welcome his tongue into my mouth, moaning when his fingers get tangled in my hair. Yet I pull away, dragging my teeth on his bottom lip before I set it free. "You said something about booze."

A throaty growl moves through him, tugging me closer as he grinds his erection into me. "We're going to have some fun tonight, aren't we?"

I nip at the air as he carries me through the hallway toward his apartment, only setting me down in front of his door. There's a voice screaming inside me, filling me with an unexpected joy. For once, the screams aren't anxiety-ridden. They're excited.

There's a mischievous grin smothered to his face, keeping his eyes fixed on mine as he unlocks his door and pushes it open. That sandalwood smell instantly infiltrates me. It's calming, it's home.

"M'lady," he says, flicking on some lights. "Mind the mess, I wasn't expecting anyone."

"I live with four roommates, I haven't seen a clean room in years." Kicking off my heels at the door, I step into his apartment which is the polar opposite of Kaylee's. The walls are a midnight-blue, walnut-stained wood covers every surface. A neon sign hangs on the wall in the dining room. And a hockey jersey rests on the wall in the living room surrounded by paintings of sunflowers and mermaids.

He's frantically cleaning the dishes off the island, placing them in the sink before he leans on the counter, watching me roam.

"Cute place you got," I say, walking my fingers on the back of the leather couch.

"Thanks."

Pointing at the framed hockey jersey. "Favourite player?" I ask.

Shaking his head, he wipes the corner of his mouth with his thumb, gaze fixed on me. "Dad used to play forward."

"You play?"

He shakes his head again, eyes scrolling over me as I lean on the island in front of him. "I can skate, chocolate ice cream is also my favourite, my birthday is in November, I don't own anything remotely this colourful, and I'm in school to be a doctor like my mom."

"Impressive."

He grins, reaching up for a bottle of whisky from a liquor shelf and uncapping it. "It's a fuck ton of work, but I want to do good in the world. And as much as I love my dad and his obsession with hockey, helping people is more my jam."

My heart swells every time, causing a smile to spread to my lips. "That's sweet."

Gulping from the bottle, he hands it to me with a nod. "Yeah, I've got a good heart like that."

"Is that where you met Greg? He's a neurosurgeon, right?" Gulping three times, I hand the bottle back and he takes another swig before placing it on the counter.

"He was my mentor for my residency."

"Small world, isn't it?"

He chuckles, eyes trailing up and down my body. "I'm not going to lie, I already knew who you were before I approached you. Kaylee talks about you all the time."

"Lemme guess, they're planning on setting us up?"

He laughs, stepping forward and sliding his fingers under my chin, tilting it upward. "Maybe, but seems like we beat them to the punch."

"Seems like it."

Licking his lips, he looks down at my chest, then back up again. "I think we should make our own version of Valentine's Day. Every year we meet up and get drunk, cursing how shitty this day can be."

Placing my palms flat on his chest and arching an eyebrow, I lean back. "Who says I'd even want to see you after tonight?"

"Who says you won't leave my bed after tonight?"

"Very presumptuous of you."

His hands slide to my hips and he lifts me, setting me down at the edge of the island. "When I heard your laugh, I knew going to that party would result in something special. And I was right. You're one special beauty, Sutton."

Hanging my arms off his shoulders, he steps closer, spreading my legs. "I only laughed because of your mismatched shoes."

"I had to bring a part of me into this outfit." He shrugs, then scrunches his nose. "Honestly, do you know how uncomfortable these pants are? Everything is stiff and tight and—"

My laughter fills the apartment, dropping my head on his shoulder. "Lemme guess, you're going to get naked and show me how *stiff* you can be."

He hums, pulling me closer to him. "I can, and you can show me you're not wearing underwear right now."

One-winged butterflies take flight in my belly, sending tendrils of urgency through me. "Take me to bed, then, Green Eyes. Show me what's hiding under all these clothes you keep telling me are too...stiff."

A husky grunt leaves him when he lifts me off the island and throws me over his shoulder. I squeal, giggling through the hallway to his bedroom as he taps my ass twice and tosses me on the unmade bed. "Beautiful."

Getting onto my knees, I run a hand through my hair and flip it over my head. "Beastly."

He yanks that pink polo over his head, dropping it at his feet. Black ink spreads across his stomach and chest. Intricate and detailed designs. But the second the button on his slacks comes undone, my eyes shift their attention to the pants being peeled off his thick, muscular thighs and revealing his hard cock underneath.

"I, too, went commando, Sutton," he says breathlessly.

Our eyes lock for an endless moment before I slide off the bed and saunter toward him, staring down at his cock as a wolfish smirk spreads to my lips. "Tell me, Lockland. Am I one-night stand material?"

His perfectly straight, white teeth rake on his bottom lip. "You're so much more than that, baby. So much more than a night I'd replay in my head daily. You're a lifetime. A milestone. An eternity."

His words wrap around me, suffocating me into pressing a soft kiss on his chest. The drum of his heart beats upon my lips.

When I remove my lips from his warm flesh, I step back until my legs hit the bed and stare at him. For all I know, he could be serious and this could be the start of something great. Or he could use me for tonight and never speak to me again.

And the way my stomach is flip-flopping, I want nothing more than to be honest and open with him. Honest to my core at how much every sentence that leaves his lips drowns me in unbridled lust.

"I love hard, break harder."

He hooks a finger in the front of my dress and tugs me closer to him, his cheeks a gentle blush. "I won't break your heart."

"How can I be so sure?"

"You can't." His exhalations wrap me in warmth as his electric stares sizzle upon my skin. "But I'm not a one-night stand kind of guy. Me and you, Sutton. We're a match made on Valentine's Day. The one day we both despise."

I don't know what comes over me, but my mouth plunders his, my tongue following suit. He rips the dress off me and lifts me again, crawling onto the bed to lay us down. Something about his need to mold us together gets to me. The kiss turns feral, biting and growling filling the bedroom; a desperate craving pulsating through us.

Pulling away from my lips, this ache forms inside me as he searches through the nightstand. But he's back on my mouth as he tears open a condom and slips it on. "There will be no one-night stands here, Sutton. Just me and you into oblivion."

My nails scratch deeply down his back, and he shudders in response. "Take me, Lockland. Show me how merciless you can be on the shittiest day of the year."

And he does, he slams his cock into my pussy, waiting a few agonizing seconds for me to adjust to his size before he's off. Every stroke, every thrust is deep and rough. He pulls out almost completely before he's back in again, repeating that movement until his rhythm is fluid, wild.

My moans bounce off the walls, setting in the silence that seeps from his apartment. And things start to build when my orgasm breaks free, climbing the base of my spine like an electric hum.

He lifts my legs, resting my ankles on his shoulders, and licks up my shin. "You going to come for me, Sutton?" My cries are desperate, I need that release. He thrusts in slow circles, biting his bottom lip as he does, and drops my legs. "I need to hear the sound you make when you come undone."

His fingers play with my clit, moving to the pace of his thrusts. My hands grip his arms, back arching, and his name chants from my mouth until I quake, shaking as the orgasm tumbles through me.

"Sutton," he moans. "Fuck, Sutton. Look at me, baby. Watch me as I come. Watch me."

And I do. I watch as his shoulder muscles flex, how his mouth hangs open and his brows pinch together. A sound like no other seeps from his lips in a breathless plea. "Fuck," he drawls. His shaking body collapses on mine. "Sutton, oh fucking, Sutton."

Giggling, I drag my fingers up his back, kissing his shoulder delicately. "I have a feeling I'm going to be hearing my name chanted a lot tonight."

Kissing my chest, he rests his head over my heart and exhales softly. "So long as no one notices we ditched the party."

His fingers delicately trace the blue veins on my chest, the tips of his fingers pebbling up my nipple. As my fingers get lost in his hair, massaging his scalp, we lay there catching our breaths.

He starts laughing, squeezing my breast before meeting my gaze and that's when I start laughing, too. His lips meet mine again before pulling away. This game was a good one. "I love you, baby."

Tapping his chest, I kiss the tip of his nose and stretch. "Mmm, I love you, too."

"I wonder if they ever get annoyed with our little games— especially games at their important life events," he asks, lying down beside me and tapping his shoulder for me to cuddle up to him. "We've been doing this since we met."

"Hey, it's our Valentine's Day tradition. I'm not stopping on their behalf."

He inhales deeply, nodding as if my words aren't what he's looking for. Lockland and I met almost two years ago on a blind date set up by our mutual friends. We hit it off instantly, but we still dislike the idea of Valentine's Day. Lockland spoils me rotten every chance he gets, but Valentine's Day happens to be the one day we don't do anything. Until we came up with this nifty idea: pretend we don't know each other and let the game play out.

It's always fun to act like someone new. But this year feels different, we didn't invent any characters. We were us, transparent and reassuring.

Lockland leans over, opens the drawer on the nightstand beside the bed, and pulls out a black bag, arching an eyebrow at me. "Close your eyes."

My eyes close and I sit up, leaning back on my heels. "Is it that crotchless lace piece I had my eye on?"

The bed shifts and something jingles before Lockland takes

my hand and rests a cold metal on my palm. My eyes shoot open and I glance down, staring at the keys in my hand. "What's this?"

"Well, you're here almost every day. You have some of your things here, your toothbrush—shit, you bought these sheets— and yet you don't live here. So..." he pauses, lifting the keyring with two keys hanging off it. "These are the keys to my apartment."

I figured this was coming, but I didn't want to say anything until he did. Although leaving my things here slowly but surely every time I came over was like subtle hints for him to get on it. And he did.

A small gold key still rests in my palm. "And this one? It's not big enough to fit into your lock."

He reaches back again, pulling out a wooden box and placing it on the bed in front of me as he gets on his knees as well. "This opens that."

The excitement coursing through me as I lift the box is overwhelming. My hands begin to shake suddenly and the key rattles at the lock before it clicks, opening the box. Inside resides another red box which he takes with a smile and opens.

"My woman, my beauty. My fucking everything. Will you promise to marry me on the one day that brought us together because of our mutual dislike of it?"

Laughter seeps from my lips, squeals and squeaks follow suit. "Are you delusional?"

"Only about you." He winks, chuckling. "Just tell me, baby. Tell me you're mine."

My eyes stay fixed on the diamond ring in his shaking hand, holding it out to me desperately. "Yes, Lockland. Yes!"

My arms wrap around his neck, bathing it in kisses. Taking my hand, he slides the ring on my finger, flashing me the most beautiful smile filled with certainty and happiness. "Tell me one more thing, baby."

"Anything."

That mischievous smirk spreads to his lips. "Will you be my valentine?"

Rolling my eyes until I see stars, I shove his face away and capture his lips, knowing that even though I believe Valentine's Day is the worst day, it just became my favourite.

THE END

ALYSSA MILANI IS an award-winning Canadian mom of two who studied at Concordia University obtaining a Major in Creative Writing and a Minor in English Literature. She independently published her first novel in 2014 of all the works that she wrote during her years at university. She now has twenty-five independently published novels under her belt, many of which are award-winners. For more information on upcoming releases and events, follow her on Instagram @alyssamilani.

BEAR TO BE WILD

MAGGIE FRANCIS

Tropes:

- Paranormal romance
- Fated mates
- Friends to lovers
- Small town

Content Warnings: one explicit sex scene, light bondage, mention of blood (not sexy).

Author's Note: This short story is set in an existing series. Our main characters are new, but some of the side characters we meet along the way have appeared in previous books.

FABLE

His weight on top of me is an anchor, the rhythm of his hips a revelation.

Powerful limbs press my body into the decadent softness beneath me and I get lost in his deeply masculine scent. He's everywhere, all at once. The ache in my core intensifies as he grips my hips in his big hands, the pressure more of a plea than anything else. A desperate request for more.

I give in to it and stretch my hands above my head, arching my back like a satisfied cat, exposing my breasts to his attention. A deep growl and then glittering heat shocks me to my bones as hot hands with rough calluses spread across my ribs, fingers I've been obsessed with for years pinch and tweak my sensitive nipples.

Yes.

I spread my legs, opening myself up to him, shivering in anticipation.

A sound registers in my addled brain, the lust and relief of finally getting him where I want him makes me giddy. I frown as I try to place the strange noise. I look down as he slowly climbs over my body, dragging his hands over my skin as if entranced. He pauses at my breasts, staring at them like he's never seen anything so wonderful before. I watch, letting my eyes roam over his hair, usually so tidy, now a scruffy mess standing up in all directions. In disarray because of my hands pulling through it in my delighted agony. Waiting for him to press his mouth over my skin.

The sound pings around me again, and I shake my head. Inhaling sharply as the sensation of teeth against my ribs pulls me back to what's happening, I look at the gorgeous man on top of me and my stomach drops into my core as he drags his tongue up the side of my breast and flicks my nipple. The tease sends fireworks through my blood. *Oh my gods.* Gasping and squirming, I want him to do it again.

His eyes darken further, the deep warm brown spreading to black as his desire bleeds through his usually calm facade. *Finally.*

I've been waiting to witness him unravel my whole life. His voice slides over my skin like warm oil as he mutters against my belly.

There is a familiarity to his words that tickles my subconscious, but I can't quite hear them. He sounds like an angel, all deep baritone and smooth whiskey smoke.

He keeps humming, the vibrations teasing my skin, but confusion sweeps icy fingers down my spine. What is he saying? Understanding hovers out of reach. Something nags at me but the heady swirl of desperate lust coursing through me makes it harder to think than I care to admit. I shake my head.

He pushes his face closer to mine, like he's thinking about kissing me.

Yes, this is more like it.

"I've got to make you understand." His voice rises, a chocolatey syrup of words that both entice and confuse the hells out of me. What is he talking about? The pressure of his body lifts away from mine and I huff in frustration. The room all around us brightens, the flickering lights making me squint. NO! We were so close to finally ruining our longstanding friendship with sex!

A hauntingly familiar melody fills the room all around me and I can't put my finger on what the *fuck* is going on. Where did he go? Why is he singing from my bedside table?

I snort and blink my eyes open. For real this time.

Oh, for fuck's sake.

Harsh morning sunlight streams into my face from the half-pulled curtains across the room. My throbbing centre pulses to the beat of my phone blaring music, the most poorly timed Rickroll of my life waking me up from what is possibly my least favourite fantasy.

Because I want it to be real.

Groaning in frustration, I grab my phone off the floor and viciously stab my finger on the stop button, silencing the dulcet tones of 80's heartthrob Rick Astley.

"Fuck you, reality. We were so close this time."

MY MORNING GOES from bad to worse as I attempt to get my unruly hormones under control. Even after bringing myself to a paltry orgasm, I've been unable to get my head out of my ass as I try to get on with my day after waking up from the sexy dream of my best friend.

The one person I shouldn't be having sexy dreams about, but who haunts my every fantasy. Evander Garcia is the sweetest, kindest man I've ever met. I've been obsessed with him since we were kids. Following him around like an imprinted baby badger, I could never stay away. He's always felt like home to me.

It wasn't until the ninth grade, when he became a tall, looming creature with broad shoulders and trim hips from swim practice, that my anchor in the world became my unhinged, sweaty fantasy. When my own burgeoning hormones shifted my feelings toward him into something darker, something dangerous. Because I can never tell him how I feel. I need him in my life, and he's never given any indication that he wants more from me than friendship.

It's even worse now since he smoothly stepped into the role of deputy sheriff in the town we grew up in. His dependable, solid roots lending themselves to the position he takes very seriously at uncomfortable odds with my wildness.

The irrepressible itch inside me to lean into mischief, chaos and the sweet siren call of the almighty shenanigan pulls me further and further from Evander's view of what's right and good and worthy. The wildness that leads me to make every bad choice I possibly can and pushes me to poke every bear I encounter. Including the one Bear I desperately wish would poke me right back.

That thought makes my mood even darker and I snarl as I stomp my feet into my shit-kicking boots and zip them up my calves. Today is gonna be a rough one.

EVANDER

Eliza Falls is out to get me, and it's not even nine in the morning.

"Jett, I know you have registration papers for her, but Beatrice can't be allowed into the grocery store. It's a health code violation." I resist the urge to rub the ache forming between my eyes and instead fold up the paperwork Jett brandished at me and hand it back to her.

"I'm her emotional support person. I can't leave her outside!" Jett grouses. Beatrice, the health code offender in question, is a miniature goat currently chewing on the baby carrier she sits in, strapped to Jett's chest. Jett stands with her feet planted wide; fists firmly planted on her hips. Beatrice's legs dangle out of the carrier, lower legs jutting straight down, tiny cloven hooves twitching occasionally. I don't think I can keep a straight face if I look at her slitted goat eyes and see the reproach there, so I close my eyes and take a deep breath.

"I appreciate that, but she still can't go into the grocery store. Perhaps you can call in your order and have Jace drop it off instead."

"Don't you take that tone with me young man. I'm here to deliver. I have event posters to put up. The Midnight Babes Association depends on the grassroots efforts of its members to spread the word on Coven events. Where is your civic pride? The annual Valentine's Day Lover's Lash is a much-anticipated ritual." Jett glares imperiously at me, stamping her foot in her heavy work boots. I let the sigh escape me this time as I recall just how intense this town gets over its holidays. The Lover's Lash is a throwback celebration to the Lupercalian roots of Valentine's Day, where would-be suitors present their desired partners with a red silk ribbon to represent the ancient custom of whipping the intended over the head with the hides of sacrificed goats. I narrow my eyes at Beatrice in her elaborate front-facing carrier. I wonder if Jett remembers that particular detail.

"Regardless of the blessed events about to unfold, the goat stays outside."

Jett frowns at me for another moment before sniffing indignantly and glaring down her nose. An impressive feat since I'm a good foot and a half taller.

"Aren't you lucky I *already* dropped the posters off." She twirls on one heel, considerably nimbler than an octogenarian ought to be, and storms off muttering platitudes to the goat.

This fucking town.

"WHAT WAS your plan before things went awry?" I maintain serious eye contact with the two young women standing in front of me, dressed head to toe in faded black lace. Lavinia and Francesca Grimshaw are identical twins in their mid-twenties who live at home in a huge old house on a hill with their younger brother Declan. They float about their days in tea-stained ivory satin and ancient lace dresses, wearing more black eyeliner than is reasonable. If there was a uniform to scream '*I want to be a vampire bride*' it would be their entire wardrobe. Appropriate considering they're living vamps.

"We were filming content for our blog," Francesca whispers, heavy black lashes fluttering against pale cheeks. Right. They're 'gothic influencers'. I don't really know what that means, but I do know they're good at it. The big old house has been in their family for generations, and in the last few years has seen a number of upgrades and repairs thanks to their online success.

"Is that real blood?"

Lavinia glances slyly at her sister, who ducks her head bashfully.

"Yes, officer."

"Ethically sourced?" I press.

"Yes, officer."

"Did you get it from Orion at the butcher?"

"No, officer."

"Do I want to know where you got it?"

The girls look at each other once more and giggle into their matching lace gloves. I take a deep regulating breath through my nose. The scent of the blood on their foreheads is definitely not animal in origin.

"I'm guessing no. But can you *promise me* no one was harmed to get it?"

They nod, more sinister giggling.

My neck prickles, but for an entirely different reason this time. Shifting slightly to let the scent of Fable Greene wash over me, I lock my knees in place to stop me from following after her immediately.

I turn back to the ghouligans. "Clean all the blood off the mausoleum before you go home." I look both young women in the eyes, wait for them to nod their agreement and then follow my favourite troublemaker.

FABLE

After hours of trying to get rid of the sexy images of Evander's big body all over mine, I'm a miserable cow. Everyone is the worst and I hate everything. Even my usual tomfoolery isn't shifting me out of my dark mood; I switched the saltshakers at the café for sugar, re-arranged all the room keys at the Bed and Breakfast, and even went so far as to sneak into the library and glamour all the audiobooks to play more Rick Astley. I haven't been able to get that fucking song out of my head *all morning* and if I have to listen to it, then so does everyone else.

But all that trickery isn't enough to make me feel better. Only one thing will, and it's the one thing I can't have. I've been dodging the very reason for my terrible attitude all afternoon. Evander has been popping into the edges of my vision all fucking day. I thought I was imagining it at first. That since I'd dreamt of him in such a deliciously devious way, I'd somehow summoned him to me. My magic doesn't work like that, but I can't help but wonder based on how often he was in my line of sight all day.

It became clear once I looped back around to watch the fallout from one of my little tricks that the blasted man was cleaning up after me. *Rude!*

I caught him talking down a gaggle of irate residents at the café after they enjoyed the surprise sweetness of their lunches. And the perfectly proportioned asshole re-ordered all the keys I'd so painstakingly mixed up at the Bed and Breakfast. He's been my shadow all day, righting all my cheeky wrongs behind me. How am I supposed to *regulate* if he keeps fucking with my hijinks?

I smile viciously to myself as I think about the glamour at the library. Only another Fae could lift that little ditty and I have it on good authority that Ulla, our town's sweet librarian and resident Fae princess, is off work today with her family.

I huff all over town for another hour before inspiration strikes like a bolt of lightning. I know *exactly* what to do to feel better.

Twenty minutes later I'm tiptoeing through Evander's living room.

Releasing some pent up frustration just being in his tidy space, I slow my steps and bring my attention back to the task at hand. I need to do something sneaky. Something he won't notice right away, so I can stew in my superiority for a little while. Being here every other day hanging out with him is one thing. It's been *years* since I snuck into his house to prank him, and the familiar rush makes me grin. Yep, this little adventure is precisely what I need to cleanse the memories of last night's pervy dream.

I slowly make my way through his whole house, keeping my glamour tight, so my lingering scent won't tip him off. His shifter sense of smell is similar to a Fae's, and this is too fun to risk a silly little slip up.

Ten minutes of wandering around offers up a delightful

reward, as I step into his bedroom and spy his side tables. There's bound to be something fun in the drawers next to his bed. I slide the first drawer open and inhale sharply at what I find inside. A well-loved leather-bound journal sits in an organized line-up with a phone charger and a pen, all tucked into their own sections of a drawer liner. *Of course* he has his bedside table organized. I roll my eyes, thinking about all the years we've spent together and how different we are. I'm a hot mess and he's so tightly wound I don't think his hair has ever been out of place. Even when we go running together, he's always immaculate.

I only consider touching the journal for a moment before closing the drawer. I love Evander and would never break his trust by reading his personal thoughts.

So, I get back to snooping through the rest of his bedroom instead.

The second drawer is the jackpot, where I find a coil of luscious red silk ribbon.

"Mmm-hmm, Evander, my precious. It looks like *someone* has a plan for The Lover's Lash this year." I've barely given myself any time to think about who he wants to lash with the ribbon and the lurch of jealousy in my heart when the front door opening sends ice skidding down my bones. Panicking, I close the drawer as quietly and quickly as possible before frantically searching for a place to hide. My heart pounds so loud in my ears I fear he can hear it from the other room.

The closet door is ajar, and without another thought, I dive inside and crouch behind the sweaters hanging above me.

EVANDER

After the longest day I can remember in a very long time, I finally managed to wrap up as much of the chaos that kept springing up all over town. Fable is mischief incarnate. I've always known this and it's never bothered me. I know she thinks it does. A lot of people have a hard time accepting her wildness. But I've always known who, and what, she is. She's a beautiful, uncouth changeling. A wild haired tempest of trickster energy, bringing beauty, chaos and uncomfortable balance to a world that sometimes feels sterile, cold and bleak.

She's also *mine*.

I've never told her how I feel about her. We've been best friends since the day we met in grade school. She was a glittering spitfire composed of sullen glares, bruised knees and grass stains. She was the most magical thing I'd ever seen in my orderly, quiet, structured life, and I couldn't get enough of her. I still can't.

Her Fae nature has always been mischief, and I know she's feeling unmoored when she sows more discord than usual. This town has its fair share of mischief makers, but the pounding headache behind my eyes and the tightness in my balls is all Fable.

I was one step behind her all day. Never actually catching up as I quietly followed behind her, righting perceived wrongs and making sure everyone was happy and safe before I tracked her to the next prank. I'm exhausted, frustrated and horny, thanks to the scent of her in my nose all day and the grin I've been fighting as I picture her glee as she set up each ridiculous situation in town. I can't let anyone know I'm actually charmed by Fable's quirks.

She's a lovely, wild creature and she doesn't need my rigid structure holding her back. She needs to be let loose upon the world like the storm she is. So she can create the change the world needs. Fable is the catalyst, and we get to watch and marvel.

My cock strains against the fabric of my stiffly pressed uniform and I'm ready to let go of some of my constraints after the day I've had. So, I clock out at the station, check in briefly with the sheriff and head home.

Fable's delicate scent slams into me the moment I step into my house, and I take a moment to let it settle over my skin as I drop my keys into the tray by the door. Kicking off my work boots and hanging my belt and sidearm on their hooks, I enjoy the memory of us here last night watching old episodes of *Buffy the Vampire Slayer* and chuckling over the mundane things we each experienced during our workdays. Quiet nights with her are my favourite. My Bear grumbles deeply in my chest, content with her scent still being in our den and I look forward to her coming over again soon so we can tuck in and let the shadows of the world slip away in each other's company. She's never more relaxed than she is during simple times spent together, our feet tangled under the weighted blanket I ordered specifically with her in mind. Her chaotic energy calms when she's tucked in tight, a gentle reminder that she's safe and secure. I don't think she even realizes it herself, but a lifetime of loving her has taught me to pay attention.

Sighing as I step away from the door, I reach into my pants and adjust myself, frustrated by the erection that springs up whenever I think about my best friend. It's getting harder and harder to keep my unrequited feelings for her in check, and I growl as the reality of my situation smacks me in the face. She would never return these feelings, and I must remind myself more and more often to rein in my own reactions to her.

Frustrated and horny, I stalk through my house and into my room. A cold shower is what I need right now.

FABLE

Evander's shoulders are *huge.*

I watch him like a creep from my hiding spot in his closet as he quietly and methodically removes his uniform. Great Gaia's tits, this male is fucking perfection. How *dare he* have those abs?!

He hangs up his uniform shirt on the back of the bedroom door and I ogle the curves of his tight ass and thick thighs while he's turned away from me. *Close your eyes Fable, stop looking and objectifying your oldest, dearest friend and respect him. Don't watch him take his pants off.*

Holy stars above.

Black boxer briefs have never graced a finer form than Evander Garcia. Lovely brown skin dusted with the perfect amount of crisp black hairs trail down the backs of the most sumptuously muscled hamstrings I've ever seen. Thick and solidly built, Evander has always been a paragon of beauty to me. Watching him efficiently remove layer after layer, putting everything in its place as he goes does something strange to my insides. I'm hot all over, the hair on the back of my neck prickling with something like panic as I crouch in the dark surrounded by the heady scent of him, the soft cotton of his spare uniforms brushing against my shoulders. What would it be like to be taken care of by him? How would it feel to let him contain some of my wild edges?

The sound of the shower starting pulls me out of my lust-addled reverie and I press my hands over my mouth to stifle my gasp. He didn't close the door and I stare, transfixed, as he slides those boxer briefs down his hips and drops them into the laundry basket. The glimpse of his ass through the crack in the door is enough to fuel my horrible, selfish brain with erotic dream fodder for *years*. Tight and round and only slightly paler than the rest of his glorious brown skin, his ass is a tribute to butt cheeks everywhere.

I nearly choke on my tongue as he turns around and I get my first glimpse of what I can only assume is the goddess's cruelest test. Time moves in slow motion, the swing of Evander's unfairly beautiful junk is barely registered by my brain, but the image of it is *seared* into my memory for all eternity. He's long, hard and sweet heavenly anaconda, I might be pregnant just from peeping at it for a split second.

Forcing my tongue off the roof of my mouth, I desperately try to pull myself the fuck together so I can sneak out of here while he's in the shower. But I just keep staring. Are those...? Yes, oh dear Lords Underhill, those are drippy, very wet soap suds I see. His very naked, wet hip grazes the side of the shower, pressing *that ass* against the side and I bite my hand to stop the shrill squeak thrumming inside me from escaping. My core throbs with unmet need and I'm breathing too heavily. I'm so horny and I'm hiding in his closet watching him shower.

Oh shit, am I a sexual predator now??

This is bad.

The shower stops and I realize too late that I'm trapped. The sound of the last drops of water falling from the shower head are thunderous as my spiraling panic battles with my unhinged libido, every nerve in my body strung tight as I curse myself for staring at the shadow of Evander's big body standing still in the shower. Why is he just standing there? His shoulders are hunched over, his chest heaving with deep breaths.

Before I can question more of my life choices, he heaves out a deep sigh and pushes the shower door open, expelling a cloud of moist air and the rich scent of him slams into me, even where I'm hiding. Being cocooned in his scent in my dark burrow, his clothes caressing my shoulders while I perv on him in the shower feels both deeply calming and incredibly deviant. My trickster magic is overjoyed to be sneaking, but my tender heart is breaking a little more the longer I stare at him. The familiar ache of knowing I'm too messy for him once more kicks me while I'm down. Literally. Crouched in his fucking closet.

I watch him in silence as he pads into the bedroom. The towel he slung low over his hips does little to hide the shape of his thick cock jutting out from his body. Knowing he's aroused right now does *nothing* to cool my own lust. I want to ride that beast all the way to heartbreak and oblivion.

I cover my mouth with my hands as he growls and flops back onto his bed, flinging the towel away from his body and I watch, utterly transfixed, as he fists his cock and begins to stroke.

Sweet Jupiter and all the stars. He's... *Oh. My. Gods. What have I gotten myself into?*

EVANDER

I can't get Fable out of my mind.

The scent of her is all around me, driving my Bear absolutely wild. Her chaos and sweet trickery fuel an adoration that started in middle school and burned into a raging inferno when my Bear fully manifested the summer we graduated and I realized what she is to me. My Ursa, my Mate. My shining star.

Keeping myself from claiming her has been the hardest thing I've ever done. But I know it's the right thing to do. Being held down by my rigid need for order would only crush her untamed spirit. And I could never do that to her. So, I make sure she's safe and let her be as wild as she needs. I'll always be here for her, and I can only hope her magic doesn't pull her too far away, so I can tuck what I can of her into my heart for as long as possible.

My cock throbs, the shower doing nothing to wash the scent of her swirling all over my den away. It's impossible to control my lust when I can scent her in every room. My Bear snarls in my chest and I throw the towel off my hips, flopping backwards and gripping myself in my fist. I need to take the edge off so I can sleep, and the only way I can do that is to wring her from my body.

I slowly pump my hand over myself, the pulsing length of me twitching as I get another wash of her scent in my nose. She is everywhere today, and I just can't hold back any more. Fisting my dick hard, I stroke myself faster, thinking about her smile, the way her hair is always in disarray and the feeling of her lean thigh pressed against mine under the blankets last night as we sat side by side on my couch.

I come hard on a groan, my cock twitching as I come all over myself. Her name slips from my lips unbidden.

I snap my head over when I hear it; a tiny gasp and a thud as something shifts in my closet. I explode into motion, leaping off the edge of my bed and diving inside as I throw the door open, nearly pulling it off its hinges. Reaching in, my arms lock around a body and I yank them out roughly, rolling them onto their back on the floor next to the bed, clasping them by the throat. I press my knee up between their legs to immobilize them and use my free hand to secure their arms above their head. Another gasp and the scent of starlight, dark places and desire slam into me.

Breath heaving, hovering over them, still dripping from the shower, it takes me a moment to comprehend who I'm looking at.

My Fable is caught beneath me, her eyes wide, pupils blown and cheeks flushed a deep pink. Her small breasts tremble as she pants, and my traitorous body reacts to having her pinned underneath me. I don't dare move, trying desperately to get my brain to catch up with the reality in front of me.

"Am I dreaming?" I hiss. My voice sounds as strained as my control. Her scent flares in the room, the little minx releasing the glamour that kept her scent from alerting me to her presence. No wonder I can't get her out of my nose! My Bear growls and I inhale sharply as her pupils spread impossibly wider. My cock twitches, hot and aching as I get hard once more.

I shift my hand at her throat, framing her jaw instead and a smear of my come touches her plump bottom lip. She breathes a ragged inhale, and then, like a fever dream, I watch her wet, pink tongue slide over her lip and *taste me*.

FABLE

His release is still hot on his hand as he firmly grips my chin, and I can't help myself. I lick my lip to bring a part of him inside me.

Groaning, my eyes roll back in my head as his flavour bursts across my tongue and I'll *never* be the same. He's salty, rich and decadent, everything about him singing to something deep inside me and I rock my hips to meet his. His eyes flare, the animal I've always loved so clear in his gaze. I want to be caged by his safe strength. I want him to press me into the floor and take his frustration out on me.

"What am I going to do with you?" His voice is thick and heavy in the tension between us.

"Whatever you want."

He stills above me. "You don't mean that."

"Yes, I do. *Please*." I strain to touch him, for my body to come into more contact. He's all heat and restraint above me and I can't stand it anymore. I pull my chin out of his grasp, catching his thumb between my teeth. Biting down hard, I watch his eyes flood to black.

"I don't want to ruin our friendship." He's trembling, his control slipping.

"Oh gods, Evander, *do it*. Ruin it. Ruin me for anyone else," I plead. I can't stop the feral whine that escapes me as he slides the hand on my chin down to circle my neck, the way my breath catches as he presses softly against my fluttering pulse. He takes a few ragged breaths, staring at me the whole time. Calculating the risks. This will change everything between us, and while there's a part of me that worries this is an ending, I *know* deep in my bones, this is just the beginning.

"I need to be in control." His voice rumbles down my body, chasing the heat that floods through my veins, pooling deep in my core.

"I know."

He pushes away from me to kneel between my spread thighs and clenches his big fist around his erection. "Take your clothes off, Fable."

I whimper and scramble out of my clothes. His eyes get darker and his jaw clenches so tight I think he might crack a molar. Until I'm naked and standing before him, trembling like a leaf, delicious anticipation thrumming through me.

"On the bed." He orders, and he waits for me to clamber on before he stretches over me to reach into the bedside table. I close my eyes in giddy surrender when I see what he's pulled out of the drawer.

With great care, Evander ties my hands together with the red silk ribbon.

He pulls it tight, anchoring me to this moment, holding my spirit to the earth and I let the tears of my joy slide down my cheeks as he carefully lifts me to my knees and uses the Lupercalia ribbon to tie my hands to the headboard so I'm facing the wall away from him.

My heart rate increases as he reverently pulls my hips back towards him, stretching my body into the shape he wants. My pussy aches, ready for him to touch me, take me, and I gasp as his hands squeeze my hips. I feel him moving behind me, his knees pushing the mattress down as he fits himself behind me, pressing his hot flesh over my own, cocooning me in his strength and scent.

"I've thought about this every fucking day, Fable. Of what you'd look like, of how you'd feel." He breathes into my ear. I moan as he slides his hands down my belly, to my inner thighs, nails dragging over my skin. He pushes my knees wide with his own. His groan rumbles his entire body and I feel every inch of him pressed against me.

"Look at you." His voice deeper than usual, his Bear riding him hard. As hard as I'm desperate to ride *him.*

"Please, Evander. I need..."

"I know what you need."

I lose all thought as he pushes his hips into mine from behind and I feel the obscene length of him for the first time. His cock is hot, long and unbelievably hard as he slides it between my legs, using my own arousal to slick along the length of him. Moaning at the sensation of his length sliding through my labia, over my clit and back again, I try to rock my hips to control the pressure, but he growls and grips my hips harder.

"I'm in control of your pleasure now."

Holy fuck.

He pulls back and licks a long line up my spine, tucking his nose into my neck as he positions his cock at my entrance once more and I cry out as he pulses his hips against me. Not pushing in, but teasingly close. I pull at the ribbon holding my wrists to the headboard, but I'm caught tight. Stretched out and at his mercy. Overwhelming sensation barrels through me as his teeth scrape along my neck, his big hands reaching forward to cup my breasts, and I let go. Let go of the need to think, to restrain the desire coursing through me and the fear that I'm too much, too messy...too wild. I surrender to this man I love, who controls my body in a way that makes me feel safe and seen and treasured.

Evander slides his hands down to my belly again to cup my pussy and I exhale raggedly when he spreads me wide with his thick fingers, spreading my slick over every part of me. The heat of his cock presses into me once more and I arch against him, pleading with my body for him to claim me fully.

He groans, the vibration of it sending thrills up my spine and begins to thrust into my tight core, gripping my hips so hard I know I'll feel it tomorrow. *I love it.* I love everything about this. He continues to pump into me, farther and farther with each stroke and I can no longer hold still. I tremble and twitch, taking every last inch of him until his full heat is pressed against my backside. He groans as he grinds his hips, the motion forcing my breasts to sway, and I clench around him.

"*Fuck*, Fable. You feel even better than I imagined. I can't, I need to..." His hips stutter and I understand what he's telling me.

"I know. Do it. Take me."

EVANDER

My rigid control shatters at her command. My senses are attuned to only one thing; Everything in my consciousness has narrowed down to the lithe wildling trembling and writhing under my hands.

This is real.

Fable, my precious, perfect Mate takes my cock so well, her body a wonderment under me and I hear only our ragged breathing. I feel only her skin under my hands. I know only this bliss.

No longer able to retrain myself, my Bear becoming untamed within me, I fuck my Mate like my life depends on it. I hold her hips above the bed, her knees no longer supporting her weight and I pull her cunt against me as I pound into her over and over. Her cries take on a new edge, her body clenching harder around me until she inexplicably *softens*, her submission complete and I snarl into the room. She throws her head back, her tumult of hair spread across her shoulders and her inner muscles tighten as her orgasm claims her body. I keep the rhythm of my hips steady as she rides out the waves of her pleasure, and a high-pitched keening, the sweetest sound I've ever heard, escapes her lips.

I let her knees down to the softness of the bed once more and untie the ribbon. I gather her hair into my fist, keeping her head pulled back. She moans and I scrape my teeth along the skin of her shoulder into her neck, grinding my hips into her the whole time. Her face is slack from pleasure, and I grit into her ear. "I'm yours. Always." Sinking my teeth into her tender skin, I explode my release into her soft body. She screams a second orgasm, the magic of the claiming bite detonating, the key to our connection turning, locking us together, forever.

The stars in my vision dissipate, the room slowly coming back into focus after my whole world flipped on its axis. Heavy breathing fills the room, and I shift my body to pull my face out of the crook of Fable's shoulder. I lick the skin there instinctively, my Bear sated and content now that we've claimed our Mate. She shivers, and I feel it in my cock, still buried inside her.

"Evander, that was..." Her mutter trails off into the bedding beneath us, and I grin.

It really was.

I don't want to separate myself from her, but my Bear demands we take care of her. I run my hands over her shoulder, down her hip, grabbing the blankets we tossed aside and cover her. I move to pull out, but she grabs my ass, anchoring me where she wants me.

"Stay."

Nodding into her hair, I squeeze her tight and press more of my weight into her. She sighs, a sweet chirrup of pleasure and my heart thuds heavily. She's radiating joy and it's all I can do not to crow from the rooftops like a smug peacock.

A sense of overwhelming *rightness* sinks into my bones. Fable's energy is calmer than I've ever felt it before, her thrumming chaos enveloped in the loveliest shroud of peace and contentment. My Bear rumbles deep, the vibration of it shaking the bed.

"There's my big guy." Fable chuckles and I can't help the answering grin that spreads across my face.

"I never allowed myself to dream that I could hold you like this," I say softly into her hair. "But now that I have you, I'm never going to give you up."

Fable gasps. "What did you just say?"

THE END

MAGGIE FRANCIS WRITES paranormal romantic comedies. What's that you ask? Why it's a lot like if Buffy The Vampire Slayer and the Gilmore Girls had a sexy lovechild. We're talking hunky werewolves, sassy witches and a cast of other supernatural side characters that make you laugh as you witness the shenanigans they get up to and enjoy the banter that comes along with an overactive imagination.

Maggie started writing as a way to joyfully escape into a world where magic is real, heroines save themselves and heroes come with a tall side order of Yes Please. Eliza Falls is a place to let the worries of the world fall away and let the romance of a fated mate and the cozy connection of a found family swoon you off your feet.

Maggie lives in Victoria BC with her own Happily Ever After, a couple of rad kids and a doodle dog. When she's not writing her next ridiculous romp, she's hunched over her jewellery bench like a sparkly gremlin listening to inappropriate podcasts and dreaming up beautiful things. You can learn more on her website, www.magpieandember.com.

INEXPLICABLE PINK TULLE

L.E. WAGENSVELD

Tropes:

- Contemporary romance
- Nerd and cool guy reunited
- Forced proximity
- Instant attraction

Content Warnings: kissing, passive remarks about alcohol and divorce.

I'VE ALWAYS HAD a knack for getting myself into . . . situations. Call it my people-pleasing nature or the fact I have no backbone. Whichever way you paint it, I do things I don't want to do or am too busy to take on. I do so because I want people to like me—for example, the grad reunion planning committee. An (almost) unanimous decision was made that I, Piper Key, would be solely responsible for planning the ten-year reunion of the Sulivan High Class of 2014. I was the only one who didn't agree to this. Since the motion was passed, however, I didn't see the need to consult any of my classmates when I decided the event should be held on February 14th. Come on, how cute would it be? We could meet the spouses of the people we'd spent years avoiding; everyone could dress fancy, sip champagne (*cough* prosecco *cough*), and dance until they dropped. It would be THE perfect evening. Or... so I thought. And I, apparently, thought wrong. Very. Very. Wrong.

Fighting tears, I stand in the middle of the dance floor, staring out at the setting of so many hours of personal torture when I was in high school—the gym. It looks gorgeous at the moment. Unrecognizable, with swaths of dark, flowy fabric draped to hide the ugly walls and torn basketball nets. Even the funky smell is masked by the subtly scented rose candles flickering around the room. The committee assured me, 'Yes, of course, Piper, we will all pay you back the night of the event. Thank you so much for taking this on' when I paid out of pocket for everything.

Well, here we are, the night of the event, and I am alone. I don't mean a few people are scattered around, and no one is talking to me. I mean, I am *alone.* There is no other living soul in this school aside from me. Even the janitorial staff isn't meant to arrive until after the reunion wraps up. It is getting harder by the second to not totally freak out. I swear, if a door creaks open somewhere, I might pee my pants. I briefly consider turning the music back up but decide I'd rather have a warning if someone sneaks in and murders me. Maybe I'll hear their shoes squeak against the floor and be able to defend myself. That image cheers me a bit—five-foot-nothing Piper Key throwing right hooks in her pink tulle gown.

I want to leave this place with a ferocity that gnaws at my bones, but I can't because, surprise, surprise, the insurance is in my name, and someone is supposed to be here until midnight. I glance at my phone. It is 9 pm. This time, I can't stop the tears that pool and spill down my cheeks. Who cares if I ruin my makeup? There is no one here to impress. Rolling my shoulders back until my boobs threaten to jailbreak from the strapless corseted top of my stupid, stupid dress, I force air into my lungs. There is a literal feast here, and it isn't like me to waste food. I doubt I can put away a buffet spread meant to feed two hundred people, but damn it, I'll die trying. I can see the headlines now:

Piper Key, 28, was found deceased in the school gym. She appears to have eaten herself to death, inexplicably dressed in pink tulle.

It wouldn't be such a bad way to go. And it would mean I'd never have to speak to any of those assholes on the reunion planning committee again. I'd just stuffed a third prawn into my mouth—I decided to start there because they'd spoil first, obviously—when it happens. Like every childhood horror movie, the echoing *creeeaaakkk* of a sticky door reverberates around me.

Oh shit, here comes the pee.

Crossing my legs, I chew faster, likely resembling a manic chipmunk. I don't want to choke on a gluttonous mouthful of seafood before I have a chance to scream. A weird keening sound makes its way around the masticated food when the gym door pushes all the way open, causing harsh fluorescent hall light to spill in and suffocate the carefully curated ambiance. A tall figure, backlit and indistinguishable, pauses in the frame. Scrambling around, I place the food-laden buffet table between myself and the door, forcing myself to swallow, though my throat is suddenly desert dry. I snatch a baguette to brandish in preparation for a fight.

"What the hell. Where is everyone?" The voice is low, the type a romance author might describe as rumbling. It's also vaguely familiar. I squint, trying to bring the man's face into focus.

"Is this…" he steps further into the room, and the door swings shut, bathing him in dancing golden light and shadow. His dark hair is shaved along the sides, longer on top and swept back off his face. Dark-framed glasses sit on his nose, and I wish I could place him. If he's here for the reunion, I must know him, right?

He shakes his head, clearly confused. "Is this the grad reunion?"

"Yes." The word squeaks out of me like air squeezing from the pinched neck of a balloon. I clear my throat, cough slightly on the remnants of a prawn, and say, "Yes, it is. You're officially the one and only guest."

He stands still momentarily, head swivelling as he takes in the gym. Then, glossy black shoes shriek against the floor as he moves closer, stopping a few feet away from me. One brow raises at the sight of the trembling baguette in my hand. "That's not true. You're here."

"I don't count," I say, shrugging as I step around the table. He cocks his head, and as he does, the candles grace his face with enough light that I can finally see him.

Holy shit. It's him—*the* guy from high school. Y'know, that person we all have. The one we ache to have notice us while simultaneously praying they never notice us.

Harrison Locke.

He hadn't known I existed. He'd been everything I wasn't. Popular, athletic. *Hot.* My friends joked we were destined for each other, given our last names: Locke and Key…come on, the perfection! The hitch in their plans was this: Harrison had no idea who I was. I ran with the library crowd, the nose-in-her-book, pushing-her-glasses-up-with-one-finger, hiding-behind-thick-bangs girl. If life were a rom-com, Harrison would have noticed me, but not until I attended a party with contacts installed in my eyes, hair blown out and glistening, a skin-tight dress displaying my as-of-yet-unrevealed curves. Unfortunately, life is not a rom-com, and I spent my existence from grades nine to twelve desperately loving Harrison Locke from the shadows.

"How could you not count?" Harrison asks, head tipping as though he genuinely cares about my answer. "You're here, aren't you? Where is everyone else?"

"Well, I organized this—" I sweep an arm, indicating the room and praying a boob doesn't pop out of my ridiculous top. "Disaster of a reunion."

"I swore the invite said it started at 7 pm. I'm a bit late, but didn't expect to miss everyone."

"You didn't." I nibble my lip before realizing I'm chewing off all the expensive lipstick I splurged on and letting it pop free. To my shock and the instant fizzing delight of my nether regions, Harrison's eyes drop to my mouth. For a moment, I forget what I'm about to say. Then, the words manage to untangle themselves from the trainwreck in my brain. "You didn't miss everyone," I splutter. "No one else has come."

The smooth brow furrows. "You've been here all by yourself for two hours?"

"Just me and this table full of food." I try to keep the bitterness out of my voice but fail miserably.

"So, wait. Let me get this straight." Harrison pushes his hand back through his hair, almost as if he is stressed on my behalf. A few of the dark strands jump free of whatever product he's applied and fall forward to brush against the wings of his brows. "You planned this event, organized all this, and no one else came?"

"Yes, that is correct." I cross my arms across my strapless chest, feeling exposed and suddenly like I might burst into tears. That would be ridiculous. I blink hard. "Are you hungry? There is...so much fucking food," I finish the sentence on an exhale of breath.

Harrison chuckles in response, and the sound lights a glowing ember of pleasure in my chest. I've never heard a more beautiful laugh or been the one to coax it free. It is a giddy sensation, and I desperately wish to do it again.

"Yeah, I'm starved," he says, pressing one hand to the flat

plane of his abdomen. As if my words are all the permission he needs, he leans around me and snatches a pickle spear, shoving it into his mouth in one go. "I got off work, threw on this suit, and came straight over."

So...Harrison Locke doesn't have a job that requires a suit. I'm instantly, insatiably curious. I imagine us sitting down, eating, drinking the copious amounts of booze I have presumably paid for, and chatting long into the night. I've come a long way from the insecure little girl I'd been, but I'm not exactly brimming with confidence. When I get ready for my job as a copyeditor in the morning, the face peering back at me is heart-shaped and sweet. I have dainty features, and though it is a rare man who would deem me "sexy," I've been called pretty, beautiful, and, on one memorable occasion, "squishably adorable." I'm still on the fence about how I feel about that one.

We don't care about those labels, remember? You are you with a beautiful soul through and through. It doesn't matter what Harrison Locke or anybody else thinks.

But that little pimple-faced teen inside me stands up and waves like *hello...it matters to me.* I mentally shove her back into her seat and step away from the table so Harrison can grab a plate. Do I "accidentally" huff in a whiff of his sandalwood and sage scent...yes. I am only human.

"Did you already eat?" Harrison wiggles his heaping plate in my direction.

"I...sort of." I grab a plate off the stack and place random items on it. I may as well join him. He'll leave after, and I'll be stuck here alone until midnight. We set our food on the nearest table, and Harrison drops into a seat, digging in with the gusto only a starving man can display.

"Do you want a drink?" I gesture to the bar, but he shakes his head.

"I don't drink."

"Oh." Well, this makes my plan of downing five glasses of bubbly a little awkward.

"You can, it's fine." Harrison notices the look on my face. "I don't have any problem with being around it."

"You certainly didn't in high school," I quip before clapping a hand over my mouth.

Did I seriously say that?

To my staggering relief, Harrison only releases a gust of laughter. "No, I didn't. It's actually why I don't drink now. My parents went through a rough divorce. There was a lot of fighting, custody battles, and all sorts of shit throughout most of my teens. I turned to booze as a coping mechanism. Things got pretty bad. I went to rehab when I was twenty, and I haven't had a drink since. I spent a long time making amends for things I did in my youth, and I don't want to be the person who uses that as a crutch ever again."

We both sit there, staring at our plates. I'm not sure who is more surprised by his confession. Finally, I swallow. "I'm sorry you went through all that."

"I don't remember you." The words are blunt and honest. A little out of the blue, but not unkind. That answers that, then.

"I didn't think so. I flew pretty far under the radar."

Harrison shakes his head. "No, it had nothing to do with you or who you were. I had my head so far up my ass, I barely graduated." He's quiet for a long moment, rhythmically chewing and swallowing. Waves of embarrassment roll off him when he finally asks. "What's your name?"

I resist the urge to drop my face into my palm. Introducing myself would have been the logical next step after him saying, 'I don't remember you.'

"Piper, Piper Key."

Harrison's mouth tips as another small huff of mirth escapes him. "That's so weird, my last name is Locke."

"I know," I mumble.

Duh! I sat in the same row as you at graduation. Our names are next to each other in the alphabet. Seriously, not even the vaguest recollection? Locke and Key?

I don't shout out any of the sarcastic words that pile up in my brain, though. He looks remorseful, and I do not wish to grind salt into a wound long healed.

"What is it you do now?" I ask instead.

Harrison sets his fork down and scratches the end of his nose before looking up at me. "I'm a social worker."

"Oh," I say stupidly. I think it's the sort of response he expected, the way he hesitated to answer. I expected him to say athlete, cop, or lawyer...and realize I am being just as sexist as the people I rail against when the girls and I have too much wine. "That's a great career, but it must be hard sometimes?" Where has this chatty version of Piper come from? I had only been alone in this gym for two hours, not a deserted island for a hundred.

Harrison's eyes drop and, if I'm not mistaken, blink rapidly before he forces out one word. "Yeah."

"Sorry," I say in a rush. "I didn't mean to pry."

Harrison shakes his head, and another strand of hair breaks free. "You weren't...I just had a tough day today." His voice breaks on the last couple of words, and a bolt of alarm shoots through me. His breathing stutter-stops as he pulls it into his lungs. I press a hand over my mouth, unsure how to react. And damn my empathetic heart, the tears, so recently close to the surface, rush to fill my eyes.

"Sorry," he says, cementing how Canadian we both are. "I maybe shouldn't have come tonight. I thought socializing might help, but maybe it would be better if I were alone."

Oh no, please don't leave.

I ache to koala bear onto his ankles and beg him not to leave me in this place. But how can I deny his escape when he seems close to tears? I open my mouth to tell him, but what comes out is, "Do you need a hug?"

Harrison's red-rimmed eyes rise to mine. "You want...to give me a hug?"

Umm, yeah. That's basically all I wanted from years fourteen to eighteen.

He stares at me for a long moment, the adult version of the boy I dreamed about for so many years, and grants me a soft, slow smile. "I'd actually really love a hug."

Heart fluttering in the base of my throat, I stand, brushing down the wild waves of my dress. Coming around the table, I fight the urge to hide my chest with my arms or to try to fold in on myself and make myself small. That's something I'm working on in therapy.

Harrison pushes to his feet, pausing, and when I open my arms, he steps into them with another shaky breath. I have to stand on my tip toes to wrap my arms around his neck. His arms come around my waist, tugging me closer after a second. Close enough, the heat pouring off his body melts through the layers of unnatural material and caresses my skin.

The aroma of his skin drifts through my blood like smoke. I squeeze a little tighter. He does the same. I don't know what has happened to this man today, but my instincts tell me he is barely keeping it together. An overwhelming urge to care for him swells in my chest.

When he swallows thickly, I allow my fingers to travel up and cup the back of his head, applying gentle pressure. Harrison emits a little groan, leaning further into me. That's fine; I'd happily live in this moment for the rest of my life.

I can't say when the vibe changes—when it goes from a comforting hug to something *more...*

All I know is that when Harrison Locke finally begins to shift out of my arms, I am aware something is *growing* between us.

Even in the candlelight, I see the flush bleed up his neck and spill over his cheeks. When he tries to step out of my arms, I don't let him. Some horny, long dormant side of me wakes up, and I tighten my arms. When his eyes drop to my lips, and two straight white teeth begin to worry at the bottom swell of his, I lean in. Harrison's strong fingers meet the column of my neck and smooth up its length before burrowing into the knot of hair at my nape. Our lips brush in a tentative stroke, a quest for permission.

Neither of us pulls back. We only pause before diving back into each other.

Harrison's mouth dances with mine, the perfect balance of soft and firm. He tastes like herbs and the sweet tang of the punch he's drinking. In some alternate dimension, teenage Piper's head is exploding.

Harrison Locke is kissing me. And it is the kiss that ends all kisses. Move over, Wesley and Buttercup.

What feels like an eternity trapped in a second passes, and Harrison pulls back, his ragged breaths brushing the heated skin of my face and my swollen lips. "I...I'm sorry, I shouldn't..."

"Oh, you very much should have." I don't give him a chance to finish, not wanting him to disparage what happened. Even if I never see him again, I will cherish this moment as the perfection it is for the rest of my days. "That kiss turned this disaster of an evening into something exciting and beautiful."

Harrison's eyes are soft as he gazes down at me. "Kissing a gorgeous girl was not on my radar tonight, but I'm also not sorry." He traces a crooked finger over my cheek, mouth curving. "And thank you for your kindness."

I shrug a shoulder, trying not to squeal and stomp my feet over the fact he called me gorgeous. "I'm a giver. What can I say."

To my surprise, Harrison laughs and sweeps an arm around the gym. "I can tell."

Groaning, I drop my face into my hands. "Don't remind me. If you hear a faint shrieking, it's the sound of my credit card imploding."

Harrison blinks, and then a slow flame of rage ignites in his eyes. "Wait a damn second. You *paid,* too?"

I bite my lip, wincing as I nod. "There was a fund, but it wasn't much. The committee told me they'd pay me back tonight."

"This is...is bullshit!" Harrison growls, and something about how the word falls from his mouth tells me he isn't a swearer.

Again, this is a real juxtaposition with the guy he was in high school.

I shrug, unsure what to say but still touched by his rage.

"No, Piper, this isn't right!" He steps away and begins to pace around, reminding me of a caged wild cat, all flowing movements. More graceful than any human man has the right to be. "I'm going to do something."

"No—" I reach for him as he passes, snagging a muscled forearm with one hand...*Oh, hello...Crap. Focus.* "You don't have to worry about it. It isn't your problem. I should have stood up for myself."

A gust of air leaves him, and he deflates slightly. "Maybe, but that doesn't make what they did right. They used you. I can't stand users."

We face each other, and I'm unsure what to say. He is flushed with annoyance at the people who aren't here to receive his chastising. His anger on my behalf leaves a glow in my chest as bright as the one kindled when he called me gorgeous. I ache to reach forward, seize the collar of his shirt and bring his lips back to mine.

"Maybe I should go," he says after a moment that stretches around us like melted sugar at a taffy pull. My heart plunges into a spiralling freefall toward my toes at the words.

"Okay." I force myself to say, even though it is one of the hardest things I have ever done. I give up hope right then and there until...Harrison's eyes drop again, the barest flash of movement, to my lips.

"Do you want..." he pauses and clears his throat.

Yes. Yes, I do want! Sir, you don't even need to finish that sentence.

"Do you want to get out of here? Maybe grab a tea or something?" he asks.

Damn it. My heart, which had jumped and caught the dangling strand of hope his words extended, hung for a second before once more plummeting. "I can't," I whisper, every trace of my sadness evident. "I have to stay here until midnight."

Harrison's mouth, all the sexier now that I know how it tastes, quirks. "Or what, you'll turn into a pumpkin?"

I give a soft snort. "I'm not sure that's how that goes."

"Let me guess, you've taken responsibility for some sort of liability thing?"

I nod, "You bet—the insurance. The janitorial staff doesn't get here until midnight. Someone is required to be onsite until then, and guess whose name is on the policy." I raise my hand like the dork I am.

"Then I'm not going anywhere." Harrison hooks his foot around the leg of a chair—without looking, the magician—scoots it over and sits.

"You really don't have to. I'll understand if you want to get out of here," I say.

Don't leave me. Don't leave me. Don't leave me.

"No way. Someone could come in and murder you."

I gasp. "Right?"

Harrison nods, then his eyes narrow as he looks at me. I may not know him well, but I don't like the expression that takes over his features.

"What?" I draw the word out.

"I know what we can do, aside from eating a disgusting amount of food."

"What?" I repeat.

"We will draft an email to the reunion committee, demanding they remove their heads from their rears and pay you your money back."

"Oh...no. I don't want to do that." I shake my head and sit back in my chair in a pink puff. "Eating disgusting amounts of food should be enough for one night."

"What if we make out more after you do it?" Harrison says, his voice dropping into a register that makes my insides fizz.

I scramble my bag off the back of the chair where it is hanging and whip my phone out. Harrison rewards me with a deep belly laugh, and I grin back at him, fingers poised like I'm ready to type.

"No, no." Harrison waggles, long, delicious-looking fingers in my direction. "Give that to me. You can dictate while I type."

"I don't know what to say."

"Say what you feel."

I purse my lips, staring at him through narrowed eyes. "Nope, I don't know how to do that," I say after a moment.

"I'll harass, coerce, and role-play with you until you do."

"Role-play?" I murmur, making a show of rubbing my chin thoughtfully.

Harrison's eyes twinkle, and he bumps his knee against mine. "Be a good girl and write the email, then we will see where the evening takes us."

Oh, I can be your good girl, Harrison. Take off your pants, and let me prove it!

I don't even recognize the sound that comes out of my mouth. Was that...a giggle? A snort? Who is to say... The main thing is Harrison doesn't recoil.

"You drive a hard bargain, sir." I bite at my lip, thinking. "Okay. I would say, Susi—"

"Susi Woods? Oh, I hated her!" Harrison growls out the words, and my mouth gapes open. "Sorry, sorry," he says.

With no small physical effort, I snap my jaw closed. "Of course you remember *her*," I mutter. Again, the reward of his smile fills me with adrenaline.

"Okay." Straightening his shoulders, he pushes his chest out and pretends to toss hair over his shoulder. "Pretend I'm Susi. What would you say?" He bumps my knee again but this time, leaves his pressed against mine. Heat fizzes from the point where our bodies touch.

"I would say, Susi, I don't appreciate how you all foisted this reunion's planning off on me. And I also don't appreciate the puke-inducing credit card bill I will receive. You and the committee assured me you would reimburse me, and yet I was left alone in a smelly old gym for two hours before the very handsome Harrison Locke showed up to suck face with me."

Harrison has to pause his typing, nearly dropping my phone as he shakes with laughter.

Over the top of his chuckling, I add, "Fuck you very much. Love Piper."

"Spectacular!" Harrison announces. "Sent."

"What!" I shriek, grabbing for the phone. He holds it above my head, laughing hysterically as I attempt to climb him like a rabid squirrel. "I'm jok—" The device slips through his fingers, and he grabs it. It falls again, and he fumbles, managing to snatch it; as he does, a familiar *Sshhh* sound fills the air. The sound an email makes as it flits off to travel through the ethers and find its recipient.

"Ohhh...shiiiittt." Harrison draws out the word in a low whisper at the same time as I gasp out a strangled, "NOOO!!"

We both stare down at the screen until it dims and goes black. "Did you just..." I whisper, my voice incredulous.

"I did. I am so, so sorry, Piper!" He presses both hands against his cheeks in the iconic Kevin from *Home Alone* pose and has no right looking so adorable doing it.

As I look into his shocked, apologetic eyes, I smile. Because, for once, the words I really wanted to say are out there. They will reach the person who deserves to hear them, and maybe that's okay. Perhaps it is time I grew a metaphorical pair...which, don't get me started on the stupidity of that saying...

As I look at grown-up Harrison Locke, still looking horrified, I realize if the shit storm that was this reunion hadn't rained down upon me, I wouldn't be here with him now.

A sudden swell of laughter bubbles inside me, like cola in a shaken-up bottle. The lid pops open, and I'm laughing. Then, I surprise us both again by throwing my arms around Harrison and bringing his mouth to mine. He gives a hum of appreciation before sweeping his tongue over the seam of my lips, seeking entrance. I give it willingly. I'm not a one-night stand person or a girl who flirts quickly and often, but I feel lit up by his presence. Like, his energy is an extension of my own, and I don't have to suffer through the awkward pressure of the small talk that usually comes with being around others.

Long fingers traverse the sides of my neck in feather-light sweeps, and I shiver. When they reach the swells of my breasts, straining against the corseted top, Harrison releases a shaky breath against my lips, and I melt. Seriously, where is that cleaning staff? They're going to need their mops to get me off this floor.

"You're so beautiful," Harrison whispers, leaning back enough to sweep his eyes over me. "In this candlelight—" he shakes his head as if speechless, and I try not to gape at him.

"This dress is hideous," I say, my voice coupling between a laugh and a whisper.

"You're wearing a dress?" Harrison says, and I lean against his broad chest and laugh. "Is it midnight yet?"

"If it were, would you come home with me?" Seriously, who is this girl, and what has she done with Piper?

"If that's what you want. I...I want to spend time with you. Take you out, get to know you. If you also want that, I mean..."

I swoon and die a little at the sight of his cheeks turning pink. Pushing my fingers into the thick hair at his nape and digging them deep, I relish the little shudder that moves through him. "I would absolutely love that," I breathe.

When his mouth clashes back with mine, it's desperate, as if our agreement was the permission he needed. My body is a livewire shooting sparks in all directions when he yanks me tight against him, and I can feel how much he wants me.

I'm not sure how long we stand, bathed in candlelight and the scent of roses mingling with the faint tang of gym socks, but it was long enough for me to fall at least halfway in love with Harrison Locke...or rather, back in love.

We are devouring each other, a mess of hair and roving hands, Harrison's erection trapped tight between us, when a harsh flood of lights spears through our corneas. We both gasp and recoil like raccoons disturbed from their trash feast by blinding headlights.

I spin to find two men holding brooms and mops, staring at us wide-eyed and open-mouthed.

"Uhh..." I say, oh so intelligently. "Please help yourself to the food. We will...get out of your hair." Threading my fingers through Harrison's, I snag my coat and purse off the back of the chair and yank him toward the door. He follows willingly, and when we finally break free into the crystal cold of the February night, we draw in deep breaths and start to laugh.

"Hey, Piper Key," Harrison says, tugging my arm so I spin to face him. "Happy Valentine's Day." Then he kisses me right out where anyone and everyone can see us. In some other dimension, teenage Piper drops to her knees and weeps with joy.

THE END

L.E. WAGENSVELD is the mother of four human children, four furry ones, and the wife of her best friend and biggest supporter. For as long as L.E. can remember, she's been a passionate wordsmith. From crafting poems about her pets as a child to the piles of unfinished manuscripts in her cloud, writing has been a lifelong necessity. In 2024, she was the grand prize winner of Dragon Blade Publishing's Write Track contest for historical fiction. She is currently the author of eight books in various genres. Find out more about her at www.lewagensveld.com.

JUST FOR TONIGHT

BECKY TZAG

Tropes:

- Contemporary romance
- Strangers to lovers
- One-night stand
- Instalove

Content Warnings: one explicit sex scene, oral sex (not explicitly described), mention of a deceased parent.

Author's Note: Just For Tonight is a prequel of sorts to *Just Friends with a Prince,* the first book in my *Just Love* series.

Cara is the sister of Harper, the FMC in *Just Friends with a Prince*, and this is the story of how she met her husband. Theo is from Sova, the fictional country I created.

While you do not need to read one to enjoy either story, they do complement each other.

"Late again," I mutter into my cosmopolitan. I shouldn't be surprised. My two best friends are anything but punctual. You'd think I would learn and arrive a good ten minutes after our meeting time but nope. I continue to ensure I'm at least five minutes early. I busy myself by studying the decorations. The subtle touches of pinks and reds the restaurant put up to celebrate Valentine's Day.

"Excuse me, can we get another round?" a deep voice to my right asks.

And fuck me if that voice doesn't immediately make me wet. A slight accent, sounding French, but not quite, in the sexiest baritone voice I've ever heard. I swear I felt his words rumble through me.

"You got it," the bartender replies, immediately getting five glasses down and pouring scotch into them. I may not be an alcohol connoisseur, but that bottle came from the highest shelf, and if reading billionaire romances has taught me anything, it's that that's the good stuff.

The man turns to me. "Umm, hi," he says. "How are you?" he asks awkwardly.

And that's when I realize I've been staring. Because this man is hot. And beautiful. Can a man be both? Whatever, I'm going with yes because this guy definitely is. He's sexy and kind. Gorgeous and nice. Not sure how I know these things, but there's something about his eyes. Christ, I'm not even drunk and I'm having these thoughts.

"Hi," I squeak. Fuck my life. "Sorry, I'm awkward and weird. Ignore me."

"That would be like ignoring the sun. Impossible." He winks and I choke on my drink. Did he really *wink* at me?

"You're pretty smooth, but I bet your girlfriend would prefer if you got back to your table seeing how it's love day and all."

"No girlfriend."

"Wife?"

"Nope, don't have one of those either."

"Boyfriend? Husband? Cat?"

"None of those. I'm all alone."

I pointedly look at his five drinks. "You don't look very alone to me."

"Hey, Doctor Morteau, where are our drinks?" a man calls out from across the restaurant. A doctor? Well that explains all the expensive scotch.

"I guess that's my cue to leave," he sighs. He expertly picks up all five glasses, and I marvel at the size of his hands. God, imagine the things he could do to me with those? I shake my head. Nope, not imagining those things because this is a stranger, men are stupid, and I'm here to hang out with the girls tonight. He takes a step away from me, but stops, puts the glasses back down on the bar, and then turns to face me. "This is incredibly bold and unlike me, but is there any chance you'd want to ditch whoever you're meeting and join me for a drink instead?"

My mouth goes dry. I'm unable to form words. I'm stuck between running away and jumping him. "I umm, I..." I trail off.

He runs his hand through his thick, dark hair. "Never mind. It's okay. Enjoy your date, I hope he treats you well. I better bring them their drinks before they storm up here." He picks the glasses up again, the fingers of his right hand gripping three of them, his left hand holding the other two, and walks away from the bar.

I stumble off my stool, reach out, and grab his arm. Bursts of electricity work their way up and straight to my chest. My eyes meet his, finding them as shocked as I feel. "What's your name?"

His tongue darts out to lick his lips, before sucking the bottom one in. "Theo. And you are?"

"Cara. And I'm here to meet friends. I got dumped two days ago." I wince at that admission. Telling him I'm *damaged goods* wasn't my plan.

"Then he's a fucking fool. You are the most beautiful woman I have ever seen."

My heart begins beating erratically, my breaths come short

and fast. My hand is still wrapped around his forearm, and all I want is to pull him close, eliminate any space between us.

Movement at the front of the restaurant catches my attention, and my two friends, Brinley and Lorna, walk in, waving at me until they notice Theo, then it turns to some inappropriate gestures.

"My friends are here," I whisper.

"My colleagues are waiting," he whispers back.

"Bye, Theo." I slowly take my hand off his arm, releasing one finger at a time.

"Bye, Cara." After another few seconds, he continues on his way back to his table, a chorus of cheers going up when the men he's with get their drinks.

"Cara! Who was that?" Brinley asks as soon as she reaches my side.

"His name is Theo, I think he's a doctor, and we talked for all of three minutes."

"Pfft, that was not talking," Lorna scoffs. "That was eye fucking. You should absolutely go back and fuck him for real."

"Umm, no," I say, settling back on my stool. "I just got dumped, I'm not looking for a new relationship."

"Who said anything about a relationship?" Lorna asks. "I said you should fuck him. Have a one-night stand. It's Valentine's Day, you deserve to get reamed."

I roll my eyes. "Nope. Not tonight. Tonight is about us."

"Really? Cause if someone as fine as that man hits on me, I'm leaving you ladies behind," Lorna says. At our raised eyebrows, she adds, "Sorry, but it's true. I love you two, but I also love orgasms."

"Whatever. Sit down and order a drink," I tell them.

We chat about work and our families. Brinley says she saw my ex and yelled at him across the street for me. I laugh hard as Lorna gives us way too many details about her most recent sexcapades.

"Cara?" Brinley interrupts. "He's staring at you."

I can feel it. Heat at the back of my head. I've felt his eyes for a while now. I turn my head slightly over my shoulder to peek at him, and there he is. His dark brown eyes laser focused on me, his finger tracing the rim of his glass. His other hand in a fist on the table. I let my eyes travel down his body, smirk, and then turn around to face the bar again.

"Damn, Cara, you just turned me on," Lorna whines.

"Oh, please. A fucking pickle can turn you on," I joke.

"Ah, Cara? Now he's coming over here," Brinley says, slapping my thigh.

"What do I do?" I say, flustered, feeling myself turn red.

"Be cool! Be cool!" Lorna panic-whispers back. Like that's helpful, I have no idea how to be cool under normal circumstances.

"Ladies," Theo's smooth voice slides over my skin. "I wanted to say goodnight. I'm heading up to my room." His eyes flick up toward the ceiling. He's staying at the hotel the restaurant is part of. He takes my hand in his. "Cara, it was lovely to meet you." He leans down and presses a seductive kiss to my cheek, before whispering in my ear, "Room seven-nineteen."

Theo strides away, leaving me flushed and fanning my face. I look from my friends to Theo's back, who is now almost to the elevator.

"Go!" Brinley yells at me, frantically waving her hands. "If you don't follow that man, I will disown you."

I glance back to Theo who is pressing the button to call the elevator. "I'll text you two later tonight," I promise, gathering my purse and downing the rest of my drink.

"No, you won't. You text us tomorrow afternoon, when you get home after a good dicking down from that man. Now go!"

For the second time tonight, I scramble off my chair and chase Theo. I run out of the bar and make it into the elevator just before the doors close.

"Hi, Theo."

"Hi, Cara."

Before I can process it, Theo has me pressed against the wall. I grab him by the back of his neck and pull his face to mine. Our lips meet in a rush of need. It's sloppy and frenzied, and so fucking perfect. His hard cock presses into my stomach and I moan at how good he feels. His hands roam my body, grabbing my ass and breasts, before he finally settles on cradling my face, while the other hand hitches my left thigh around his waist, bringing us closer.

The elevator dings and the doors slide open. Theo pulls away just enough to speak. "If you've changed your mind and would rather go home, now's the time to tell me."

"Does it seem like I've changed my mind?" I roll my hips into him.

"I need to hear the word *yes*, Cara."

"Yes, Theo. I want you so badly," I admit before kissing him again.

"Thank God." He kisses me back and then picks me up. I giggle and wrap my legs around his waist. Theo marches us down the hall, stumbling a bit as I kiss and nip up his neck and across his jawline. I hear the click of the door being unlocked, but don't unwrap myself from his body. He walks us straight over to the bed, where he tosses me down. Fuck that was hot. Theo doesn't waste time. He has his shirt thrown off and is unbuckling his belt. One-handed. That move has me more turned on than I've ever been.

"Enjoying the show?" he asks, grinning, making a dimple appear. Theo is a large man. Broad shoulders and back, thick thighs, muscular arms. Dark chest hair I want to run my fingers through. He doesn't have a six-pack, but he's fit. He's wider than any man I've ever been with, and the errant thought that he'd be a good cuddler pops into my brain, but thoughts like those don't belong in one-night stands.

I prop my cheek on my palm and openly ogle him. "I really am."

"I've, uh, I've never done this before," Theo says, looking

around the room, avoiding eye contact with me, his cheeks turning an adorable shade of pink.

"What? A one-night stand?" I ask and he nods. "Okay, well, do you want to stop?"

"No, God no," he says, shaking his head vigorously. "I just wanted you to know that this isn't typical of me. I don't go on business trips and hook up with random women before I fly home."

"Theo, it's fine. I knew what I was getting into when I followed you into the elevator," I tell him.

"I leave tomorrow. This is just for tonight. As soon as we part ways, we'll never see each other again." A look passes over his face, but it's gone in the blink of an eye.

"Well, if this is just for tonight, then let's not waste any time." I sit up, pull my shirt off, toss it at his feet, and unclasp my bra, letting it fall away from my body.

"Fuuuuck," he says, his eyes going wide as he greedily takes me in. "Pants," he orders.

"You too," I say, motioning to his unbuckled, yet still on, jeans. Theo grins as he unzips his pants and shoves them down his legs. I follow his lead and shimmy mine off, keeping my underwear on, just as he has.

Theo joins me on the bed, the mattress dipping under his weight as he settles his body over mine. Our lips meet, crashing together in a force so strong it feels beyond our control. We kiss and explore, working each other into a craze.

"Cara," he croaks out. "God, I can't even think. I...fuck, you're so sexy."

"Then don't think. Tonight is about feeling, being in this moment, just us. And also," I murmur against his lips. "You're so fucking sexy. I can't wait for you to be inside me."

Theo groans and then pulls me by the back of the neck, holding me in place as he fucks my mouth with his tongue. I slide my hands down his body, marvelling at the way he shudders beneath my touch.

I don't stop until my hand is under his boxers and I grasp his thick cock in my palm. I moan at the feeling of it. God, how I love the feeling of a dick in my hand, and this one might be the most perfect one of all.

"You need to stop or you're going to make me come, and I'm not done with you yet," Theo growls into my neck.

"Oh, don't worry, we're just getting started. You said just for tonight, not just one time." I wink at him playfully.

Theo responds by pulling his body away from mine, and just as I'm about to protest, he slides his body down, wrenches my thighs open, pulls my underwear to the side, and slowly licks me from back to front, sucking my clit into his mouth hard. I scream out and grab a handful of his hair.

"Fuck, Theo. Just like that," I mumble.

"Pull my hair," he moves away slightly to say, then sucks on my clit again.

"What?" I'm too lost in pleasure to understand his request.

"Pull my fucking hair. Hurt me, Cara," he begs. "I had no idea I liked that, by holy gods, did that fucking turn me on. Hurt me. Use me. Pull my hair and leave marks on me, please."

I do as the man asks and grab a fistful of hair and tug. Theo growls into my pussy, making me feral. "Make me come, Theo. I need to come."

Theo plunges two fingers inside my soaking cunt, licking and sucking my clit as he pumps them in and out of me. He doesn't stop, he fucks me hard with his fingers, and I love it. I love that he's not gentle with me. He gives it, and I take it. My thighs clamp around his head before I explode around him. I shake and scream and see fucking stars. I haven't orgasmed that hard in a long time, and damn did I ever need it.

"That was the hottest moment of my life," Theo says, climbing up my body. "Seeing you come was a fucking religious experience." Theo kisses me again, and the taste of myself on his lips makes me wild with need. I push down his boxers and he chuckles against my lips. "Want some help?"

"I need you inside me right now, Theo. Right. Fucking.

Now." I pull my own underwear off, kicking them away as soon as they're at my ankles. As Theo takes his off, I bend down to pick up my purse and retrieve the condom I stuck in there just in case.

"Put it on me," Theo says, giving his cock a few slow strokes. I lick my lips as I watch him. "See what you do to me? I met you an hour ago, and I'm completely out of my mind for you."

I rip the package open and roll the condom on his cock. "Your dick is so fucking perfect." The admission falls from my lips as I stroke him. "You're so thick."

"Glad you think so. Now lay back and let me in." Theo lines himself up with me, sliding the head of his cock along my pussy, then he grins devilishly and thrusts into me as hard as he can. "Fuck, Cara. Holy fucking shit!"

"You fill me so well," I moan. "No one's ever felt this good."

"Cara...this is...I can't..." Theo closes his eyes and shakes his head. He doesn't say anything else, but I understand what he means. Nothing has ever come close to feeling like this. He's been inside of me for all of thirty seconds, and I can already tell this is the best sex of my life. We fit. Physically, yes, but there's also something more, some magical chemistry between us that I can't allow myself to focus on because this is a one-night stand, just for tonight.

Once Theo moves again, we don't stop, we can't stop. Hands and tongues and lips are everywhere. He fucks me hard and I match his pace. No more words are said, moans and grunts are all we can manage. Theo kisses his way down my neck, until he reaches my breast. He sucks my nipple into his mouth. I arch my back and rake my nails down his back.

"Make yourself come. I want to watch you get yourself off around my cock."

I do as he asks, running my hand down his side, slipping it between our bodies. I grasp the base of his dick, squeezing it and feeling him move in and out of me. I glide my fingers through my wetness that's coated his cock before pressing on my clit. My pussy clenches around him, making him groan against my breast.

It doesn't take me long before I shatter, coming again by some miracle that only this man can provide. Theo releases my nipple with a pop, and I grab his head between my hands and pull his face up to mine again. I kiss him roughly, still coming down from the high of my second orgasm.

"Come inside me, Theo. Now. Fuck me as hard as you can," I say, shocked I'm able to string a sentence together.

And he does. He slams into me over and over again, so hard I won't be surprised if I find bruises on my body later. He comes with a roar, his head nestled in the crook of my neck. I bite down on his shoulder, screaming at the intensity of the moment.

We lay together for a few moments, our chests rising and falling as we both attempt to catch our breath. Theo eventually raises up on his elbows and brushes the hair out of my face with both his hands.

"Hi, Cara," he whispers.

"Hi, Theo," I whisper back.

We clean ourselves up, and as we're putting our clothes back on, Theo clears his throat.

"You know," he says. "You still look pretty tired. It's probably not safe to be walking around on jelly legs."

I bite my cheek to stop from smiling. "You're right. It would be a safety hazard. I don't want to fall and hurt myself."

"It would probably be safest if we got back into bed," he says, and then adds, "For safety."

"For safety," I agree.

We climb back on the bed, this time settling on our sides facing each other, pulling the comforter over our bodies.

"You mentioned you're here on business?" I ask, wincing as I pry, knowing full well this isn't one-night stand protocol.

"Yeah. I was here for a conference. I'm an endocrinologist."

"And where are you from? I can't figure your accent out." I've been trying to all night but can't place it.

"Sova," he says. I must have my confusion clearly written on my face, because he chuckles. "It's a small country in Europe, between France and Spain."

"Ah, right. And you leave tomorrow?"

He searches my eyes. "My flight is at three tomorrow afternoon."

Which means we'll have to say goodbye soon. But not yet. "Tell me about Sova."

We talk for hours, laying in that bed, our legs intertwined and our gazes locked. We trail our fingers over each other's body, and kiss lazily and sweetly. We talk about our childhoods and families. He tells me about his large, sometimes overbearing extended family, and I tell him how hard it was for me and my sister after my mother passed away when I was a teenager. I talk about my cousins and aunt and spending our summers together at the cottage. I explain how close we all are, and that our cousins feel more like siblings to me and Harper.

We fall asleep at some point after round two, and I'm jolted awake from the sound of a closing door down the hall. Theo's already awake, his bright eyes taking me in as the early morning light breaks through a gap in the curtain.

"Hi, Theo."

"Hi, Cara."

"I guess I should get going," I say slowly.

"You need a shower," he blurts out. "To start your day, you should have a shower."

I bite my lip. "And we should also eat breakfast."

Theo presses his lips to my forehead, the sweet gesture almost bringing tears to my eyes. "Yeah, we need breakfast too." He scoops me up out of bed and carries me to the bathroom. Theo sets me down and turns the water on, testing it first to get the right temperature, then we help take off each other's clothes. As soon as we're in the shower, we're kissing frantically again. The hot water rains down on our bodies, making them slippery as we grope each other. I run my fingers over the scratch marks on his arms and back, while he licks at the hickeys on my breasts and neck.

Theo presses my back against the tiles where he kneels and kisses his way down my stomach until he reaches my pussy. He licks and sucks and bites until I'm a convulsing mess against him. My orgasm hits me fast and hard, and he has to keep me from falling over. Once I'm stable, I pull him up, spin him around so he's backed up against the wall, and lower myself in front of him.

I stroke him slowly, watching as he tips his head back and groans, his Adam's apple bobbing up and down. I lick the head of his cock, the salty taste of him making me moan. I take him as far down my throat as I can and suck hard. I work my mouth up and down, kneading his balls at the same time. Theo grabs a fistful of hair, tugging on it, making me grin. I work his cock faster, needing him to come. Theo chants my name before his body goes rigid and he shoots his cum down my throat.

After I lick him clean, we stand under the water, taking turns to wash our hair and rinse off. We haven't stopped touching. It feels wrong to not be touching him in some way, which is fucking stupid because he's about to get on a plane and be thousands of kilometres away, and besides, I barely know this guy. Instalove isn't real. This is simply a reaction to the amazing orgasms he's doled out. I'm high on endorphins, that's it.

We dry off, Theo helping me squeeze the water from my hair, before we start getting dressed. I open my bag, pulling out a pair of panties.

"Do you always travel with an extra pair of underwear?" Theo asks.

"Not always, but you never know when you'll need them," I say. "And it's a good thing I tossed in a pair last night because I really don't want to put that back on." I point to the pair I was wearing yesterday. Theo picks them up, smirks, and then puts them in his suitcase.

"Did you just steal my thong?" I ask, shocked at the move.

Theo shrugs. "Yep. Let's go get some breakfast."

I lead Theo to a hole-in-the-wall diner that serves giant stacks of pancakes and bacon that is always cooked to the perfect crispiness. We share more stories from our lives growing up over mediocre coffee. After the waitress clears our plates, and we've lingered longer than the staff would probably like, we slowly walk out of the restaurant.

"What time do you need to leave for the airport?" I ask him.

Theo glances at his watch. "Probably in an hour." He looks at me again with those warm, brown eyes. "Do you have a car, or need to call a cab, or?"

"I have a car. I parked at the hotel last night," I say quickly. I'm desperate to stay with him for even a bit longer, thanking the universe that we have this short five-minute walk back to the hotel together.

Theo grabs my hand and laces our fingers together, squeezing tight as we walk down the street. An antique store has a few tables outside and I pull Theo over to it.

"Look at this locket! It's so pretty." I pick up a vintage silver heart locket with an ornate matching key, each on their own separate silver chain. There's a tag keeping the items bundled together that reads, *Your heart is yours, but give the key to the one you trust the most to keep it safe.* I smile and place the locket back down, giving it a gentle brush of my fingertips as I move on to the next table to see what else the shopkeeper has.

After a few minutes of browsing, Theo joins me again and we continue our way back to the hotel. He walks me to the car, where I take my time digging my keys out of my purse.

Before I have the chance to overthink it, I ask, "Do you want a ride to the airport?"

"I..." he trails off, biting his lip and looking at the clouds. "Yeah, I really would, Cara."

We go back into the hotel and grab Theo's bags, then check him out before heading to the airport. We drive in silence, neither one of us wanting to admit out loud that this is it. I pull into Pearson International Airport's parking garage, not even considering simply dropping him off and driving away. Once parked, Theo grabs his bag from the trunk, and we walk hand-in-hand into the airport. I go as far as I can with him, clutching onto his hand for dear life.

"I have something for you," Theo rasps. "Just a little something to remember our night together." Theo reaches into his pocket and pulls out the locket I was admiring.

"Theo," I say, shocked at the antique necklace in his outstretched hand. I carefully pluck the necklace out of his palm, but make quick work of taking the tag off and separating the two chains. "I want you to keep the key. That way you have a bit of me with you, too." I hand him the second chain, and in silence we put on our new necklaces.

Theo grabs me in a tight embrace, his arms around my shoulders, with one hand cupping the back of my neck. I have my arms around his waist, pulling him as close to me as I can. He kisses the top of my head, and I fail to keep the tears at bay. I had hoped I could make it back to the car before breaking down, but that clearly didn't work out.

"I'm never going to forget you," Theo says into my hair. "We might have only had one night together, but you'll forever be in my heart."

I nod against his chest. "I don't want to say goodbye to you," I admit in a hushed tone. "This wasn't supposed to mean this much, but Theo, in less than twenty-four hours, you've managed to become more important than I could ever have thought possible."

Theo kisses the top of my head, then my forehead, and finally my lips. This kiss is slow. Sad. It's a kiss that is desperate to keep going, even though we know it must end. Both of us are crying, there's no hiding the tears or emotions we're feeling. I hold his shirt in my fist over his heart, and he continues to cradle the back of my head. We stay like that for a few minutes, drawing out the inevitable.

"I have to go," he whispers.

I nod. "I know."

I pull him down for one more kiss, and then he's walking away from me. His head is down, his shoulders are hunched. I can't seem to get enough oxygen into my lungs, I'm gasping for air as I watch him walk away.

He's just about at the gate that will lead him to international departures when he stops and turns around. I run at him, launching my body into his arms.

"I don't want to say goodbye," I say, looking into his beautiful eyes, still wet with unshed tears.

"This isn't goodbye. It can't be goodbye." He smooths the hair from my face, tucking a wayward lock behind my ear. "This is the beginning for us, I know it. We were meant to find each other."

"I think so too. I refuse to say goodbye to you."

"So we keep in touch, do the long distance thing?" Theo's eyes search mine.

"Yeah, for now. I only want to say hello to you, not goodbye."

He smiles. "Hi, Cara."

"Hi, Theo."

"Think you'll ever want to come see me?"

"Yeah," I breathe. "I think I might like to come to Sova one day."

THE END

BECKY TZAG WRITES spicy romance and drinks more tea than you. She calls her stories hot hallmark — they're cozy, low angst, will make you happy, and they'll also give you some happy pants feelings. Learn more at linktr.ee/beckytzagauthor.

LIFT TO LOVE

ROCHELLE WOLF

Tropes:

- Contemporary romance
- Workplace romance
- Forced proximity

Content Warnings: kissing (not extremely explicit), mention of claustrophobic spaces (trapped in elevator).

As the elevator rattles and turns dark, Aimee Hartman's only thought is that she can't believe she's about to die single. Using her phone's flashlight and a rationality that she's often commended for here at King Street PR, she presses the Call Help button.

Nothing.

"Damn," she hears, muttered behind her. Aimee whirls around to find Joelle Stevens peering back at her with a raised eyebrow. The other woman grimaces, likely because Aimee's light is directed right at her eyes.

"Oh, sorry." Aimee quickly lowers it.

Getting stuck in an elevator with her office crush is not what Aimee had planned for Valentine's Day. To be fair, she doesn't actually have plans. Other than maybe watching a rom-com and pretending that next year would be her year. So as far as plans go, that would certainly have been more depressing, but perhaps not as scary.

"It's okay. Usually I'd offer to help, but I'm not quite sure what there is to do in this situation. The elevator here is creepy enough without this added bonus. I swear, I flinch every time it rattles between floors 29 and 30..." Joelle trails off and blushes.

"I'm glad I'm not the only one who notices that. Everyone in Marketing thinks I'm imagining things."

That draws a genuine smile from Joelle, one that Aimee has only ever seen directed at other people before this. It almost stuns her.

"I'm Aimee, by the way," Aimee adds, realizing she's probably staring a little too intensely at the other woman.

"Joelle," Joelle says. Aimee has to resist the urge to say "I know."

Realizing that help probably isn't coming any time soon, Aimee removes her winter jacket and drops her bags to the ground, moving closer to Joelle as she does so. Just so they can hear each other better, of course.

"Good idea," Joelle says and does the same.

This is the only conversation they've ever had, and Aimee doesn't know what to say next. She's used to having office crushes, people she would pass in the hallways and wonder what department they worked in. She would imagine somehow ending up together in a supply closet, the obscure object they're looking for located on a high shelf, their hands brushing as Aimee passes it to them... Then the moment would pass and Aimee would go back to thinking about the next TikTok she needed to film for a new client and she would never think about them again.

Except, Joelle...somehow Aimee hasn't been able to shake her. In the few months that they've been working on the same floor, Aimee has never had a chance to talk to her directly. They'd be cc'd in emails together, always as people who needed to be "kept in the loop," but that's the extent of their relationship, if one can even call it that.

"Sorry, is the flashlight annoying?" Aimee asks after a minute, painfully aware of how slowly time is moving. How long does it take to fix an elevator anyway?

"No, it's convenient. Thanks. It's probably the only thing that phone is good for now anyway. It's so annoying how we get no service in these things."

"I know. I can't believe how little time has passed. It's so creepy, I can't believe *this* is how I'm spending Valentine's Day."

"Because being trapped in here with me is so horrible?" Joelle's question has an obvious jokey tone to it, and Aimee laughs.

"It's not the company. Well, it's the *company*. The organization. I already spend too much time here as it is."

Joelle hums in agreement and slides down to the floor, sitting cross-legged against the elevator wall.

"Sorry, I'm getting tired. May as well sit if we're going to be here for awhile."

Aimee nods and then spends far too long thinking about where she should sit. Would sitting next to Joelle be weird? Should she sit across from her? She decides to just sit against the nearest wall, next to the elevator buttons. She experimentally hits Call Help again, but it remains unlit.

Joelle sighs. "Don't buildings like this have backup generators? What is going on…"

Aimee can't help but repeat the sigh, making Joelle turn to her. She tilts her head curiously.

"So, what big Valentine's Day plans did you have?" Joelle asks. It's a natural enough question, but the hopeless romantic in Aimee wants it to be Joelle's subtle way of asking her if she's single. The situation is so close to what Aimee might have imagined, she has to remind herself that sometimes questions are just that: expressions of simple curiosity. Or, in this case, a way to pass the time.

"Nothing, actually. It was going to be a normal after-work day —just some TV time and maybe some phone games. What about you?"

"Same here. Maybe order some heart-shaped pizza just to feel like I'm doing something."

Aimee laughs. "I've never tried those, though I always see the ads for them. I'm curious about how the slices would work."

"That's a good point. I never thought about the pizza-eating logistics. I'm pretty partial to a triangle slice myself."

"I'm pretty sure you're wrong. Everyone knows the best pizza slices are the centre of a party size pizza. No crust is the way to go."

"You're dead wrong on that. The crust is one of the best parts. The crust with a little bit of creamy garlic dip is what dreams are made of," Joelle says passionately.

"Well, you can have my crusts then," Aimee says, shaking her head.

"I'll hold you to that if we get out of here alive," Joelle responds, and though Aimee can't see her very well, she's hoping the smile she's picturing is actually there.

Before Aimee can ask if she's being serious, the elevator jolts and the lights flicker on. The sterile white lights are such a contrast to the previous dimness that Aimee has to blink a few times to reaccustom herself to their glare. She reaches over from her spot on the floor and presses the ground level button, and the elevator begins beeping and moving slowly downward.

"Wow, that was quite the ride," Joelle says, standing up and brushing off her black slacks.

"Mm-hmm," Aimee responds, clearing her throat. The sudden jolt had scared her more than she wants to admit, and it's taking all of her composure not to reveal it. Her heart is beating wildly, and she forces herself not to press a hand against her chest.

"See you next week, yeah?" Joelle says, grabbing her stuff off the floor and shrugging on her jacket. Aimee stands and nods. When the elevator doors open, Joelle calmly walks out, brushing past the waiting security guards.

"You okay, ma'am?" one asks as Aimee gathers her jacket and purse off the floor. She nods at them as she walks out, still not trusting her voice enough to speak.

Taking her phone from her pocket, she puts her headphones in and turns on her calming playlist. *Phew.* No ordinary Valentine's Day indeed.

AFTER REHASHING the story to her closest friends—including Lisa, her work bestie, who's appropriately horrified and thrilled— and an abridged version to her parents (no, they don't need to know that her dying thought was about how she didn't want to die single, thank you), Aimee comes up with a professional way to tell her manager that she'd like to work from home for the next little bit to recover. Her manager, bless her heart, is extremely understanding and even sends her a "you got this" gif over Slack, which is more sympathetic than Aimee anticipated.

Always one to make the most out of a less-than-ideal situation, Aimee spends the next few days coming up with new content pillars for her clients, planning out video ideas, and even finding a few new organizations that the company could pitch their services to. But now it's Thursday, and with nothing left to do other than the actual filming, Aimee has to go back to the office.

Waiting in front of the elevators, she stands back so other people can make their way up. Deep breath. *You can do this, Aimee.*

"Heading up?" says a familiar voice behind her.

Aimee can't tell if the sudden dryness in her mouth is down to relief or nervousness. Joelle looks as effortlessly confident as ever, already holding her winter jacket and showing off her tasteful sky-blue suit.

"Yes, if I can steel my nerves," Aimee admits, exhaling heavily through her mouth.

"Oh, is that why I haven't seen you around this week?"

I can't believe you noticed, Aimee wants to say, but she settles on the much more socially acceptable response of "Yeah, I've been doing some work-from-home days. I've been a bit nervous about having to use the elevator again."

"Totally fair. I took Tuesday off. I was a little freaked out yesterday, but I think I've got the hang of it now. Why don't we go together?" Joelle asks.

Aimee is unsure how to respond to this simple gesture of kindness and understanding. She was half expecting Joelle to tell her to just get over it, like Aimee has been telling herself. To hear that her feelings are valid is more affirming than she expects.

"That would be nice," Aimee manages to say.

She follows Joelle, and soon they're pressed against each other in the crowded elevator. It's always like this before 9am in a building in Toronto's downtown core, and when their hands brush as the elevator begins its ascent, Aimee doesn't pull away, and neither does Joelle.

THE *PING* of an incoming Slack message pulls Aimee away from the virtual meeting she's zoning out of. She's on mute, her manager handling most of the talking with the client. Aimee is usually only there to take notes and confirm that everything the client is saying is part of their existing marketing strategy, and this meeting is a walk in the park; Aimee has had the content perfected for weeks now. When the meeting ends, she'll have to head out to the site to actually film, so her manager is confirming that the client has all the props and set space they need.

JOELLE STEVENS: Hey, how's your day going?

Oh my gosh, are they on messaging terms now? Aimee has to school her face so it appears as if she's still paying attention to the meeting.

AIMEE HARTMAN: Good, sorry I'm in a meeting

JOELLE: Oh my bad, I didn't mean to pull you away, it's nothing

Oh no no no. Aimee *has* to know what Joelle wants to talk about. It's a need as strong as the one for cold water after a long walk in the Toronto summer heat, a cool sip in an otherwise insufferable humidity; she needs to know as if her life depends on it.

AIMEE: The meeting is just wrapping up, don't worry about it

AIMEE: How's your day going? Any finance stuff my team needs to adjust for yours?

There, that's a safe question. Work appropriate, even.

JOELLE: Day is also going good. Thankfully no mishaps from Richard - though I wouldn't be surprised if something came up, it is quite early

Aimee has to resist the urge to laugh. Richard always messes up their invoices, and it usually requires Joelle's intervention to fix them.

JOELLE: But I didn't say that

AIMEEE: Of course not. I'll keep an eye on him

JOELLE: Thank you

JOELLE: Anyway, what are you doing for lunch? <*pizza gif*>

Aimee has never been more grateful to hear the words "Thanks for a great meeting, bye" before. She manages to smile and tell the client that she'll see them soon, and when the meeting closes out, she immediately returns to the message.

Oh, how she wishes she wasn't about to get a catered meal. As much as she wants to skip this client lunch, they've been so lovely and kind to her, and she really is looking forward to meeting them. The more she gets on their good side, the more likely they are to keep hiring King Street PR, and as much as she hates this part of her job, bringing in clients is part of what she does.

AIMEE: I wish I was free. I actually have to head out to see a client

AIMEE: Maybe next time? 🙏

JOELLE: Of course, next time then 

The message is accompanied by a gif of someone doing a thumbs up, and Aimee swears her heart grows three sizes. This could just be innocent friendliness, but for now, she'll allow herself to see it as flirting.

IN THE DAYS THAT FOLLOW, no more messages from Joelle appear in Aimee's inbox, and as much as she wants to reach out and invite Joelle to lunch, something always keeps coming up. Between juggling all her clients' new product launches and making sure her teammates feel seen and heard and appreciated for the work they do, she hasn't had a free moment to herself, not even for lunch.

She debates inviting Joelle out for a post-work meal, but she's not sure their relationship—whatever it is—is at that stage. Would it seem too much like a date? While Aimee is not one to put up with ambiguity or avoid confrontation in her professional life, in her personal life, she keeps herself guarded. One too many misreadings into a friendship has left Aimee wary about revealing her interest in someone. However, her strategy of waiting for potential dating prospects to present themselves to her hasn't exactly worked out either...hence her sad Valentine's Day plans.

Now Aimee stands in front of the entrance to the large open floor space King Street PR owns on the 68th floor of the building. The end of February seems like a weird time of year to throw a party, but it's the company's way of celebrating their employees before the busy season starts. Not only will the finance team soon be swamped, but so will Aimee's content creation team as their clients firm up their own financials and realize they actually have extended budget for the next fiscal year. (Or worse, they *don't* have the budget, and then her team will have to spend the next few weeks hustling for new clients.)

Either way, this party is usually regarded as the big event of the year, and everyone, from the CEO to the interns, lets loose a little.

Amy exhales, then walks in. The noise from outside the room was loud, but muffled, and she still finds herself confused by the cacophony of sound that hits her.

She makes a beeline for the bar that's been set up for the event, smiling politely at the other people in line. She's just wondering where Lisa is when said work bestie appears, as if conjured by thought.

"Whatcha getting tonight?" Lisa asks, drink already in hand. "The corporate mixed beverages are actually kind of good this year. I'm surprisingly enjoying this Work Hard Play Harder cocktail." She takes a sip of her drink as if to prove her point.

"Was Angelo in charge of naming the drinks this year?" Aimee asks.

The drink names and mixtures change every year thanks to the contribution of the Food & Beverage team, and this particular name has the uptight asshole written all over it. He's known around the office for being a beverage pro, but Aimee's heard too many horror stories from Lisa to have any doubts about his true nature.

"Yes, but I helped with a few. I'm particularly proud of I Can't Espresso Martini How Much I Love You. I thought it was so fun."

"I'll have to get that then," Aimee says as she gets to the front of the line, and she places an order for the drink.

Feeling less awkward now that she has her bestie and some booze, she follows Lisa to one of the many standing tables set up around the room. She takes a piece of bacon-wrapped asparagus from one of the many waitstaff passing hors d'oeuvres around.

"Good turnout this year," Lisa remarks, glancing around the room.

"That must be good for your team."

"Of course, otherwise I'd be hearing from Angelo for weeks about how we should've stuck to his menu and beverage providers. I respect the man, but his choices are always way over budget."

"Respect? Since when?" Aimee raises an eyebrow at her friend, who blushes.

"Whatever, it's not my story to tell," Lisa says, avoiding the obvious question and taking a sip of her drink.

Aimee shakes her head but decides not to press further, especially not here where they're likely to be overheard. She follows Lisa's example and looks around the party, hoping to see someone else she can rope into their conversation for some work gossip.

Her eyes stop when she spots the table full of finance staff. She can't help but look for Joelle, and she smiles when she spots her. Joelle looks stunning tonight, as she always does. Her makeup is done simply but elegantly, and she's wearing another perfectly tailored suit. This one is grey, as if she stepped out of a Saks catalogue. Joelle doesn't strike Aimee as frivolous, but her well-fitted suits make Aimee wonder about this luxury she allows herself. Before she can wonder about anything else, however, Joelle turns and spots her. Joelle's eyes instantly light up, and she smiles before giving a tiny wave.

Oh my god. Aimee doesn't know how to process this adorable display from the professional woman she knows.

"I didn't know you knew Joelle," Lisa says, snapping Aimee out of whatever staring contest she was taking part in.

"Oh, yes, our projects overlap sometimes. She's always cleaning up Richard's messes."

Lisa nods. "That makes sense. She's a lifesaver for me too. I don't know what I'd do without her."

"Right." Aimee takes a sip of her drink to remind herself that she didn't come to this party to be distracted by beautiful women. But what other purpose would there really be for an office party of this scale?

"Hi, Lisa. Hi, Aimee."

Aimee obviously can't catch a break because Joelle has appeared in front of them. Now that she's closer, Aimee can see that what she assumed was a simple makeup is actually a smatter of sparkles and glitter on Joelle's eyelids and bright red lipstick. If they kissed, would some of those sparkles fall onto Aimee?

She needs to be slapped. She needs to be taken out of here immediately. Lusting after a coworker is a recipe for disaster.

"Hey, Joelle," Lisa says, oblivious to Aimee's inner turmoil. *Good, one of us needs to be rational.*

"I was just coming over to thank you for organizing another great party," Joelle says, turning to Lisa. Of course there's a professional explanation for why she's here.

Lisa waves away the praise but blushes slightly. "Oh, thank you. You know how it is—always have to outdo ourselves."

"And you always do," Aimee chimes in, not hesitating to give her friend the compliment she rightfully deserves.

"Well, thank you," Lisa says and raises her hand for a cheers. Joelle and Aimee clink their glasses against hers, and the women sip their drinks.

"So, how are things for you in the finance department?" Lisa asks Joelle. "We were just talking about how you're a lifesaver."

Oh my god, Aimee can't believe Lisa would betray her in this way. Everyone knows that you shouldn't tell someone you were just talking about them, right?! Aimee can't tell if she's being reasonably irked or it's just her oversensitivity when it comes to anything involving Joelle.

"Things are going good. And thank you. I work hard to make sure my team can function well, but I worry that if I ever take too long of a vacation, I'll come back to exploding computers."

"I know how you feel," Lisa commiserates, sneaking a glance across the room where Angelo is schmoozing with some of the directors.

Joelle turns to her. "Aimee, how have you been?"

"Good, how about you?"

She wishes she could've come up with a great line, but Aimee has never been known as a charmer. Her previous relationships had developed naturally, a meeting arranged between mutual friends or developed over time with like-minded individuals. She's not sure what to do with the instinct to take Joelle someplace private and let her kiss her silly. Or something like that.

"That's great to hear. I know it was a bit of an adjustment after last week."

"Oh, you heard about the elevator story too?" Lisa says. "Our poor Aimee." She wraps an arm around Aimee's shoulder sympathetically.

"We were stuck in the elevator together, actually," Joelle says.

"Oh my gosh, it must've been so scary!" Lisa shivers, as if even picturing it gives her the creeps.

"It wasn't too bad. I had good company." Joelle smiles that warm, brilliant smile at Aimee, and Aimee has to make sure she's not stuttering when she replies, "Likewise."

Before Aimee can think of something smarter to say, someone yells Lisa's name from the next table over and she detaches herself from Aimee to run to greet them.

Now alone with Joelle, Aimee continues to sip her drink in a way she hopes is very demure.

"So," Joelle says, "how about that pizza?"

"Now?" Aimee can't hide her surprise.

"I have a real craving for it," Joelle says, and her smile has Aimee nodding.

THE PIZZA PLACE is surprisingly not too busy considering it's a Friday evening. Most people walk in to grab slices, but Joelle orders a large pizza for them to share. They agree on a marinara dipping sauce, even though Aimee remembers Joelle's favourite is creamy garlic. Is Joelle worried about garlic breath for some reason? God, Aimee hopes so.

They chat about work, the annoying client that has somehow managed to piss off both their teams (a rare feat considering budget and creative vision are usually in conflict with each other), the TV show that everyone in the office has been raving about ("Wait, *that's* what it's about?!" exclaims Joelle when Aimee explains it to her), and the latest TikTok trend that Aimee really wants to get the finance team to participate in.

The conversation is nice, too nice, and Aimee is struck by a feeling that things are proceeding too smoothly. She can't remember the last time she had such an easy time talking to someone she hadn't already known for years, and the lack of awkwardness between them is a refreshing change from her usual first ~~dates~~ meetings.

At the end of the dinner, when Joelle yawns and remarks it's probably way too late for them to be out on a workday, Aimee surprises herself by asking for Joelle's number.

"So we can get lunch together some time," she hastily adds, as if needing an excuse.

"Sure," Joelle says and hands over her phone. "And you can send me that TikTok video you were talking about."

"Of course...though I'm still surprised you haven't seen it. Our algorithms must be very different."

"Well, my algorithm is all lesbian dating horror stories and cucumber salad recipes at the moment, so that may be why."

Aimee reminds herself to remain calm. If that isn't an admission to what she's been suspecting, she doesn't know what else it could be.

"Mine is also fairly gay, but of the pop music kind," she says, hoping that this is a fairly normal thing to say.

Joelle nods in understanding and smiles when Aimee passes back her phone—Aimee's phone number now securely saved in its contacts—and Aimee is proud of herself for maintaining eye contact, despite the blush she feels working its way onto her cheeks. She's talked about her queerness before and she isn't shy about it, but it's different, revealing it to someone she's interested in, knowing the chance that they're interested in her too has gone from impossible to possible. It's the feeling of wanting to be seen and understood in a way that some people would never be able to understand.

They part ways with a restrained hug that Aimee initiates. She's a hugger, and casual affection among friends isn't something she's a stranger to, so she tries not to read too much into Joelle's warm pat on her back, or the way she squeezes for an extra second before she lets go.

"Text me when you get home," Joelle says, a standard farewell among those who take public transit in the city past 10pm.

"You too."

When Aimee gets home, she sends a text to Joelle. In the privacy of her home, she lets herself smile at the heart reaction she gets in response, hoping it has more meaning than just a friendly affirmation between friends.

THE NEXT DAY, Aimee has to resist the urge to slam her laptop shut in frustration. She takes a deep breath and decides to go straight to the source of their potential doom. The junior staff member responsible for the report she's reading is sitting at a desk not too far from her.

"Jasper, where did you get the budget for Sunshine Studios?" Aimee calls across to him.

Jasper looks up and seems to deflate a little at this question. Aimee is quick to reassure him. "Not that the report isn't good. It is, but I want to make sure the numbers are accurate before we run it by them. We don't want to be overbudget or it'll be back to the drawing board."

He nods and looks through his notebook. "I think from Tiana in finance. I asked her about it over the phone."

With an internal sigh, Aimee thanks Jasper and tells him she'll look into it. Those on her team know her idiosyncrasies, and if there's any kind of agreement or information trail, Aimee wants to make sure they have it in writing and possibly photographed several times. They've been saved from many a disaster this way, and it's this need for precision that now finds her in the storage room with Joelle.

The files aren't anywhere on the finance team's hard drives, and Tiana is on vacation until after the proposal deadline, so Joelle and Aimee are conducting a manual file search.

Well, Aimee is conducting a manual file search while Joelle leans against the neighbouring file cabinet, staring at her.

It's making it very difficult for Aimee to actually focus on what she needs to do.

"Are you going to help, or are you just going to keep staring at me?"

"Well, this is really a job for one."

Aimee looks away from the files to glance at Joelle. "So, you're here because...?"

"I wanted to spend time with you."

Joelle says it so simply, but the effect of the words on Aimee is anything but simple. She knows she's blushing as she turns back to her task, but she doesn't know what to do about it.

Joelle must notice too because, after a minute in which the

only sound is the shuffle of paperwork under Aimee's suddenly unsteady fingers, she giggles.

"Oh my gosh, you're so cute," Joelle says.

"Thanks, I think?"

"You're welcome. It was a compliment after all. You should accept compliments when they're given to you."

"Thank you, then," Aimee says again, and this time she looks up at Joelle. Is it her imagination, or has she gotten closer?

"So, do you want to grab dinner after work?" Joelle asks. "Something nicer this time."

"Sure." Aimee tries to keep her voice casual. "I don't have anything planned."

"I was thinking more like a date, if that's okay with you."

If Aimee wasn't already blushing, she definitely is now. She decides to try channelling some of Joelle's confidence.

"That's more than okay," she says, and her voice is hardly shaking at all. "I was hoping you'd ask."

Joelle smiles and takes a step closer. Aimee's face is practically on fire now.

"And there's a reason you couldn't ask me yourself?" Joelle's usually serious tone has lightened, and Aimee recognizes this slight difference—the difference between friendship and flirting. This question is definitely not in the realm of friendship, and if they're now flirting...

"Well, what if I like it when my romantic prospects take charge a little?"

"Hmmm." Joelle pushes the cabinet closed and takes a step closer. Aimee steps backward.

"I wouldn't be opposed to that," Joelle says, stepping forward again. Aimee's next step backward has her up against the wall, but as Joelle slowly inches closer, she decides it's not a bad place to be.

Is she about to live out her workplace fantasy? God, she hopes so. She thinks about the lock-and-key tattoo on her ankle and what the tattoo artist told her: "Trust me, people with tattoos are fearless. 'You think you can scare me? I've had my foot stabbed repeatedly with needles' is all you need to tell your intrusive thoughts."

Aimee smiles, and Joelle pauses just inches away and tilts her head.

"What's so funny?"

"Nothing, I promise. Would it be ridiculous if I asked you to kiss me?"

For an answer, Joelle closes the gap between them and Aimee is in heaven—the softness of Joelle's lips, the boldness of her kiss, the way they feel pressed up against each other.

But after only a minute of bliss, Aimee pulls away. Anyone could walk in.

"Now that I've crossed that off my dream list, could we continue this someplace less public later?"

Joelle steps back and laughs, a laugh that Aimee hasn't heard from her before but is determined to make happen again...later.

"Sure. How about I cook for us tonight? I know my way around a kitchen," Joelle says as she straightens and rebuttons her suit jacket. Did Aimee do that? Oops.

"Just a kitchen?" Aimee teases, going back to the file cabinet. Thank god she had decided not to wear lipstick today, otherwise it would now be all over Joelle's face.

"I—" Whatever Joelle was about to say is interrupted by Jasper walking abruptly into the storage room. Aimee steels her face in a neutral expression and hopes her blush has somehow miraculously gone away.

"There you are, Aimee. Let me do this; I feel so bad," Jasper says.

"Oh sure, thanks, Jasper. I was just getting started on this file," Aimee lies, knowing Jasper will need to restart the efforts because Aimee has very likely missed the relevant documents in her first scan, too distracted by Joelle's presence.

"Oh, would you look at the time?" Joelle glances at her wrist, which Aimee can clearly see doesn't have a watch. "I have a meeting in five, I should get going. See you later, Aimee."

She winks before she heads out, and Jasper, noticing it, chuckles awkwardly. Aimee rolls her eyes playfully and follows Joelle out, making sure to keep a bit of distance between them.

As she gets back to her desk, her phone *pings*.

JOELLE: See you at six in the lobby. Can't
wait to show you my way around a kitchen

Aimee hearts the message and tries to hide her smile, not wanting the rest of the office to see her get all flustered. Aimee's not sure how it all happened so quickly, but at least something good came out of that elevator fiasco a few weeks ago. Maybe next year will be the start of a very different Valentine's Day tradition: heart-shaped pizza and close encounters with a beautiful woman.

THE END

Rochelle Wolf is a Toronto-based queer writer interested in warm love stories and books that feel like a hug. They have perfected the art of making their special interest (books) their entire career. Formerly a librarian, they now run their own book editing business. Visit their website (www.rochellewolf.com) to learn more about their low stakes, cozy sapphic novellas.

GALWAY GIRL

LAURA MEREDITH

Tropes:

- Contemporary romance
- Love at first sight
- Strangers to lovers
- Unexpected pregnancy
- One-night stand

Content Warnings: one sex scene (some foreplay mentioned, but no explicit talk of sex), unexpected pregnancy.

Author's Note: This short story is a companion to *Killorglin* and *A Very Killorglin Christmas*. It takes place after the events of the latter. There may be light spoilers for them in this story, but none will ruin your experience of the novels if you read them afterward.

THE HOUSE IS dark save for the few candles I've left in the entry, living and dining rooms. The kitchen is a mess, but with any luck, she won't go in. I don't want to ruin tonight.

Tonight is too special.

The front door opens, and my heart hammers in my chest. Through the doorframe that connects the dining room to the front entrance, I see her plaid scarf being pulled from around her neck. Her long, dark hair moves with the fabric.

"Right frigid out there," she comments. "But it was nice to spend the day with your parents. Aine's excited to spend the night with them, too, though Caitriona is still heartbroken over that lad. She just went upstairs to the guest room and didn't leave. And Ronan is..." Her words trail off when she finally appears in the dining room and sees what I've done. A smile tugs at the edge of her lips as her eyes scan our table, where I've laid out all her favourite foods.

There she is.

My whole world. My Sarah. *My wife.*

I don't know how I got so lucky to share a life with her, but I know for damn sure I will hold tightly to her until I'm cold in the ground.

"Let me guess." I walk toward the most beautiful woman in the world. "Ronan doesn't want to spend the night with his nan and granddad."

I wrap my arms around Sarah's waist and pull her into me. Her eyes sparkle in the dim light, the same eyes that caught my attention all those years ago.

"How about"—I press my lips to her, and even though we've kissed countless times, it always feels like the first—"We forget about the kids, and just be us. It's Valentine's Day, after all."

She smiles against my lips, and the feel of her smile is just as beautiful as the look of it.

"Okay," she agrees.

I step away, pulling a chair out for her. She sits down as I push it in, then take a fabric napkin and place it across her lap. I then take the bottle of red wine I opened earlier and pour her a glass.

I sit across from her, taking my napkin and placing it in my lap before pouring myself a glass of wine. Sarah sits with her hands clasped in front of her mouth as she looks at what to eat first.

My wife loves pasta so I've laid out a buffet of her three favorites: carbonara, lobster alfredo, and tomato-basil bruschetta ravioli, along with a Caesar salad, her favourite side to eat with pasta.

"Dig in," I say with a chuckle.

"I want to. I'm just not sure where to start." Her hands move down to her stomach, and I feel a pit grow in mine.

Carrying four children changed Sarah's body over the years, but it seems the weight of bearing those pregnancies has nothing on the weight of the war waging inside her. She never talks about it, at least not often. It's more in the things she does that I notice it. Every once in a while, she restricts her food or jumps on some fitness trend. I always make sure to tell her that she's beautiful. In the privacy of our room, I worship her body. I murmur to her how much I crave it because I do. I crave it like a bee does honey —like a musician does a perfect melody.

I reach across the table and take her hand in mine. "Sarah, babe." Her eyes meet mine. "Do you know how gorgeous you look right now?" She looks down, and I squeeze her hand. "Darling, I'm serious. You've only grown in beauty over the years."

She takes a breath and looks at me again. "I know what you see. I wish I saw it too."

I want my words to embrace her so tightly she has no choice but to live *with* them, but maybe this isn't a moment for words. So, instead of trying to convince her, I take the closest pasta dish, the alfredo, and start scooping some on her plate.

"What are you doing?" Sarah protests, but I don't listen, reaching for the ravioli. "Babe, I'm not going to be able to eat all this."

I shrug. "Eat what you want."

She laughs. God, I love her laugh.

When I finish dishing us up, I pick up my fork and look to her to do the same thing. She does, and I can see the protective walls she put up have come down. She twirls a healthy helping of lobster alfredo on her fork and puts it in her mouth.

That's my girl, I think to myself as I take a mouthful myself.

We eat in silence. Sometimes, when you've been together as long as we have, it's not about constant chatter but the ability to enjoy each other's silence. The soft glow of the candles highlights Sarah's face. The quiet doesn't bother me. If anything, it feels as loud as talking because as I watch her eat and drink, I think back on many of the meals we've shared over the years. I hear the sounds of plates clattering while children talk over each other, trying to tell us stories of their day, and I see her smiling at me through all the chaos.

"What are you thinking about?" she asks, her lips twisted to hide a smile.

I put my fork down and pick up my glass of wine. "I'm thinking about how twenty years have gone by quickly."

Her brows rise. "They have."

"Do you ever think about how we first met?" I ask. "How we became...us?"

She laughs. "Imelda will never let me forget."

I think about my meddling sister-in-law. She always knows what's going on in the family. Just this past Christmas, she put her foot in her mouth where my brother Patrick and his now fiancée Laurel are concerned.

"Tell me the story again." Sarah breaks me from my thoughts. "I love it when you tell *our story*."

I refill her wine glass. She picks it up, takes a sip, and waits for me to tell a story she knows as well as I do. I can't help but indulge her because it's my favourite love story.

"I dreaded Puck Fair in 2004 because it meant summer was almost over. I was twenty-one, and I hated uni. I was preparing for my final year at the University of Dublin and couldn't wait to graduate. Of course, I didn't know what I wanted to do with my life when I graduated. At that point, I'd spent most of my days acting the maggot.

"I set up for the annual barn party the night before we'd head into Killorglin for the goat crowning. My brother Donal pulled up with the alcohol from his newly opened pub in Killiney along with his wife Imelda and little Colleen." I smile as I think about my niece at that age. Now she's married and trying to start her own family.

I look at my wife. She's still smiling, waiting for me to continue.

"As usual, Patrick rolled in late.

"'Hey, guys!' Patrick slid in next to Donal and me.

"The party was in full swing. The entire town of Killorglin was drinking, dancing, and otherwise enjoying the merriment of the Byrne annual party.

"'Finally showed up from whatever God-forsaken land you've been in,' Donal commented before bringing his cup of beer to his lips.

"'That God-forsaken land was Ireland,' my brother told him with a sly smile. 'Back on the ol' emerald isle trying to make some living doing odd jobs.'

"Donal let out an unimpressed *pfft* then said, 'Could've come to the bar. I need the help.'

"Patrick shook his head. 'Cause you'd pay me.'

"Donal looked at his younger brother. 'Experience is payment.'

"'I need money. I want to get over to America finally.' Patrick pulled a couple of carrots from a tray next to us. 'I'm waiting on my paperwork.'

"'Doing things more officially over there, I see.' Donal chuckled. 'No more under-the-table work. Good on you.'

"'America doesn't look kindly on foreigners who overstay their welcome.'

"'That's so far,' I complained, not really listening to the flow of conversation. I hated how spread out the three of us had become.

"Donal bought the pub, not caring that it was on the other side of the island from the farm. Patrick wanted to see the world. I just wanted life to be like it was when we worked side by side on the farm.

"'I'll always come back,' Patrick assured me. He looked around the room with a smile on his face. 'How could I ever miss this?'

"I shook my head. I doubted Patrick would ever be back once he left.

"'I have some news.' Donal's expression turned serious as he looked between us. 'You cannot tell Mom and Dad. You can't even let Imelda know I told you.'

"Patrick smiled brightly. 'I'm going to be an uncle again!'

"'That was an anticlimactic delivery,' Donal said with a shake of his head.

"Patrick wrapped an arm around the eldest of us. He spoke his congratulations in Irish Gaelic. I mumbled my own, '*Comhghairdeachas,*' but it wasn't filled with the heart Donal deserved.

"I excused myself from my brothers, my heart sinking further. I saw Imelda shaking her hips with Colleen on the dance floor. It must've been early in the pregnancy because there were no outward signs of her carrying a *wean*. Even though I was happy for Donal and Imelda, it only drove the thought that my brothers were moving on from this farm, and I wasn't.

"I needed something to dull the sadness in my heart. I saw a bottle of whiskey, swiped it from the table, and headed to the back of the barn.

"I gripped the whiskey in my hand as I climbed the metal ladder to the loft. It had always been my safe space. Anytime I was upset at Mum, Dad, or my brothers, this was where I'd run. I'd hide in the haystacks and let the worst of my anger, hurt, or sadness pass. I expected tonight to be no different, only a little louder as the party wore on downstairs. To my surprise, when I reached the loft, I heard soft crying."

Across the table, Sarah blushes. I can only imagine how uncomfortable it was for her to meet me with puffy red eyes. I saw how beautiful she was, though. I always do.

I continued the story, "'Hello?' I called out into the stacks.

"A small gasp, but no face to go with it. I knew it was a woman and didn't want to scare her.

"I looked between some hay bales, and that's when I saw her. I stopped dead in my tracks and swallowed deeply. Her pale, gorgeous skin was marred by black mascara streaks, showing the trail of her tears. It was jarring to see such a beautiful woman so profoundly sad, and even though I didn't know her name, something tugged at me. It made me move toward her.

"'Is everything alright?' I asked.

"If looks could kill, the one she gave me would've taken me out. Her eyes narrowed on me. She wiped at her smudged makeup, helping lessen the look that she'd been crying. 'Yeah, I'm doing great because appearing like I'm barely holding it together is an obvious sign of that.'

"It was hard not to smile at her comment, but I held it together.

"I sat down across from her, my back agains the haybale. I opened the bottle of whiskey and took a swig, then handed it to her. I didn't expect her to take it, but to my surprise, she did. She took a long drink. I was impressed. Most women balked at the idea of a glass of whiskey, much less taking a drink straight from the bottle.

"She handed it back to me, and in the exchange, our fingers brushed. A jolt of electricity bounced from her to me, sending warmth through my body.

"'I'm Connor.'

"It wasn't super bright in the loft, but the dimness didn't hide her beautiful pale blue eyes beneath her dark hair. God, she was so striking that I couldn't describe how I felt looking at her.

"'Sarah.'

"*Sarah.* The name meant 'princess,' and princesses always made me think of the most beautiful and elegant women, like the late Princess Diana. It was fitting for her.

"'What has you up here crying, Sarah?' I tested her name on my tongue. I liked it.

"'It's silly.' She looked down at her lap.

"I took another sip of the whiskey, then handed it to her. 'Try me.'

"She took the bottle, studying the amber liquid. Her pale eyes looked back at me, and her looks again enamored me. 'My friend came down here to look for an old lover. She found him and left. I don't know how to get back to the town from here, and if I do, she's likely in *our* room having sex with him.' She shook her head. 'Silly.' She took a sip of the whiskey and handed it back to me.

"'I could take you to town,' I offered. 'Help you find another room somewhere.'

"She looked at me, then at the bottle in my hands, and then back at me again.

"*Touché.* She had me there. I hadn't had so much to drink that I was out of my mind, but enough that I knew better than to drive.

"I wetted my lips. 'You could stay here. On the farm.'

"She scoff-laughed. 'Yeah, sure. I'll just sneak into the farmhouse and hope the family doesn't catch me.'

"I narrowed my eyes and pursed my lips like I was contemplating all life's mysteries. 'Another option is I can let you into the house.'

"Sarah opened her mouth to protest, and then realization washed over her face.

"'Oh my God. This is *your* party?'

"'My parents'. If we're going for accuracy,' I said with a shrug.

"Sarah quickly stood up, brushing pieces of hay off her. 'I'm so sorry. I know I shouldn't be up here, and—' She shook her head and made for the ladder.

"I quickly stood, abandoning the whiskey and my earlier bad mood. I reached out and grabbed her hand. It forced her to spin, and her body crashed against mine. Chest to chest, we stared into each other's eyes. I wanted to say something to her, but all the blood had left my brain and entered my cock.

"'Is that your wallet?' she whispered, and I knew she felt me.

"'No.' I shook my head.

"'Oh.'

"Her eyes trailed to my lips, and I knew I needed to take a chance. I pressed my mouth firmly to hers. It wasn't how I usually offered a first kiss. I liked to take my time and allow a few light brushes, but Sarah seemed like a flight risk. If I didn't show my cards, she would leave down into the party and off into the night.

"She moaned against my lips as I wrapped my arms around her waist. I breathed in her dizzying honey-peach scent.

"I didn't want our kiss to end. I was too scared once it did, she'd leave, and now I'd kissed her. Now, I'd made it impossible to let her go, and I wasn't used to that feeling.

"'Let me take you to the farmhouse,' I said, desperate to have her in a way I'd never felt before. I had her trapped in my arms, our foreheads pressed together.

"I felt a deep yearning for her as if she wasn't right in front of me—like holding her close would be impossible, and yet she was in my arms.

"She didn't respond, and each microsecond created an ache in my heart.

"'You can say no.'

"Her eyes met mine. 'I know. I just don't want to say no, and I don't know if that'll make you think less of me.'

"I smiled and kissed her deeply again. She giggled against my lips.

"'I did the asking,' I reminded her.

"'You can also do that taking,' she whispered.

"I didn't hesitate. We went back down into the party. I pressed my hand to the small of her back, guiding her through the crowd.

"'Connor?' I closed my eyes at my sister-in-law's voice.

"I turned and faced her. 'Hello.' I looked down at my niece, her hand gripping her mum's.

"'Who's this?' Imelda asked, looking at Sarah with a knowing look on her face.

"'This is Sarah,' I said, smiling at the woman beside me.

"'A friend from uni?' Imelda asked.

"'No.'

"Imelda looked between us. I knew she knew what I was planning to do. It was a question of if she was going to cock block me before I could.

"'Mummy,' a small, whiney voice brought our attention to Colleen. 'Mummy. Tired.'

"Saved by the niece. Donal and Imelda were staying in a small house on the property Mum and Dad normally rented out, but they were between tenants.

"Imelda smiled at her daughter. 'Alright, darling. Let's find Daddy to say goodnight.'

"My sister-in-law shot me a quick glare that I'm sure was supposed to be a message to behave myself before leaving to find Donal.

"'Let's get out of here.' I grabbed Sarah's hand and pulled her out of the barn.

"We ran across the gardens that separated the barn and house. She giggled the whole time.

"'Wait!' she called. 'I can't run in these.'

"I looked down at her strappy sandaled heels. I thought wearing them to a barn party was silly, but who was I to judge? I scooped her into a bridal carry. She squealed in delight, and I wondered if she'd make a similar sound beneath me.

"Inside the house, I pushed her against the door as I closed it. My mouth captured hers again, and everything felt right in the world. She moaned. My cock ached, it was so desperate to feel her.

"'Connor,' she said breathily against my lips.

"I growled, nipping her bottom lip as punishment for ruining our kiss.

"'I need to know something.' She pushed on my chest, forcing me to look her in the eyes. 'This is just one night, right?'

"I blinked. For some reason, the thought of only one night with her felt like a knife to the chest. As I looked at her, I also knew I couldn't pass up any opportunity to have her.

"'Of course.' I kissed her again. 'One night.'

"She took my cheeks in her hands and pulled me in for a kiss. I lifted her effortlessly, and her legs wrapped around my waist. I carried her upstairs, and I laid her on my bed. I kissed her jaw and neck, enjoying the sounds my peppered kisses elicited. My hands reached for the hem of her dress, and I slowly slid the fabric up her smooth legs.

"'I don't know you,' she said between pants and kisses.

"'I'll tell you anything you want,' I said as I crouched between her legs, and kissed up her thighs.

"'Where do you go to uni? Ah!' She cried out as I pushed her panties to the side and licked up her slit.

"'Dublin,' I answered, not wanting to talk but savour this woman and her taste.

"'I go to the University of Galway,' she said, then moaned as my tongue circled her swollen clit.

"The panties had to go. I pulled them down her legs and pushed her dress up further for better access.

"She tasted delicious. I could live between her legs and survive solely on eating her pussy.

"'Aren't you going to say anything?' she asked between pants.

"I chuckled against her. I looked up to see her expectant eyes on me.

"I licked my lips, enjoying the taste of her as I did. 'I thought this was just one night.'

"She shrugged. 'One night doesn't mean you have to be a total stranger. Say something. Anything.'

"I looked her up and down, her beautiful pussy waiting for me to finish devouring it. I moved over her, pulling her dress up and over her head, pleasantly surprised to find she was not wearing a bra. I tucked some of her long, dark hair behind her ear.

"'I'm not surprised you're from Galway. You're pretty much the picture that song painted,' I said.

"In the small bit of light from the moon across my bed, I saw a slight flush of her cheeks.

"'Anything else?' I asked.

"'Get undressed,' she instructed, and I obeyed.

"That night, I learned the difference between sex and making love. Sex has always been a way to satisfy myself physically. Making love was caring about the other person, and I desperately cared about Sarah's satisfaction. I was tender and gentle in a way I'd never been with a woman. When I finally slid inside her, I saw stars.

"Sarah, the beautiful Galway Girl, writhed beneath me as I slowly moved in and out, teasing her while at the same time reveling in the feel of her around me for as long as possible. With each movement back in, I would press a little harder.

"I moved inside her, savouring the feel of her. Each stroke. Each touch. Each kiss. It all pulled me away from everything. From reality. Until all that was left was Sarah.

"I fell asleep with her in my arms, and I'd never felt more at peace. I was shattered when I woke the next morning and saw she was gone."

My wife hums and looks down at her plate. I tilt my head. "Why do you look sad? You know this is part of our story."

She looks at me. "It's my least favorite part. I never should've left like I did."

I stand and walk around the table. I sit next to her and take her hand in mine. "But this part led to all the good stuff. So, can I finish my story?"

She takes a breath and nods.

"I wasn't surprised she left. It was only one night. I got out of bed and noticed one of the condoms we'd used hadn't made it into the bin. I picked it up and saw something that made my heart drop. The condom was broken. I felt panicked, and I knew I had no way of reaching Sarah. I didn't even know where she went or how she got there.

"My heart raced. Maybe she was on the pill. Perhaps I pulled out before I came. Though I knew I definitely didn't do that.

"I went downstairs to see Donal and Imelda sitting at the table. Colleen wasn't so much eating porridge as wearing it.

"'Mum and Dad?' I asked, going into the kitchen and trying to act normal.

"'On a walk,' Donal answered, not paying any attention to me. He kept cooing at his daughter, encouraging her to eat more breakfast.

"I pulled down a mug for coffee.

"'Morning!' Patrick's voice boomed from the stairwell.

"*Great.* I thought sarcastically to myself, it was exactly what I wanted *more family.*

"Patrick came into the kitchen, looking me up and down. 'You alright?'

"'Fine,' I grumbled.

"'No. He's not alright,' Imelda said. 'He brought home a girl last night. I saw her slip out into a cab this morning.'

"At least now I knew what happened to Sarah.

"Both brothers looked at me wide-eyed.

"A sly smile spread across Patrick's lips. 'Do tell.'

"'Nothing to tell,' I said. 'It was a one-night thing. I'll never see her again. I need to go pack for school.'

"With that, I left. I went to my room and busied myself, getting ready for school. I had to. Every time I stopped, I thought of what I had found that morning and the woman who had no idea.

"There was a soft knock on my door.

"'Come in.' I assumed it was one of my brothers, hoping to get more information. I mentally prepared myself for battle. I didn't want to share my night with either of them. They'd cheapen the most intimate moments I'd ever shared with a woman, and I couldn't have that.

"'Connor?' It was Imelda.

"I cleared my throat. 'How can I help you?'

"'I'm wondering if I can help you.' She sat on the edge of my bed, scrunched her face, and then moved to the chair at my desk. 'You seemed off downstairs.'

"I sighed. Imelda had always been perceptive. She could read between lines that other people couldn't see. I adored her. I always had. We'd shared a special relationship, and she was like the sister I never had growing up. I could trust her with difficult things. She knew I wasn't happy in Dublin and that I felt directionless. My brothers also knew to a degree, but Imelda took the time to try to help me understand my feelings. I knew she'd do the same here as well.

"'If I tell you something, can you keep it a secret?'

"'As long as it won't cause harm,' she answered.

"I thought about it for a minute. It could. A broken condom could mean an STI or...

"I swallowed. I looked at my sister-in-law's stomach, then back at her.

"'Oh God. Donal told you.' She threw her hands up.

"'Don't be mad. He's excited.'

"'Don't tell your mum and dad.' She pointed her finger at me.

"I drew an X over my heart.

"She repositioned herself in the chair, then said, "Now tell me what troubles you.'

"I took a breath. 'The condom broke.'

"Her eyes widened. 'Oh God. I thought you were just heartsick. This is so much worse.'

"She wasn't wrong about the heartsick. 'I have no clue where she is.'

"'*Shite*.' Imelda shook her head. 'What are you going to do?'

"I shrugged. 'Go back to school.'

"'Connor!'

"'What else am I going to do? It's not like there's some fancy internet place I can search for a Galway girl!' I knew I shouldn't yell at Imelda. She was only trying to help.

"'Myspace?'

"I waved a hand. 'Nothing will come of it. I'm sure I'll never see her again.'

"Imelda looked about as certain as I truly felt. She rubbed her knees, then stood. 'Okay. Well. Killiney isn't far. You know where to find Donal and me.'

"I nodded. She walked over and hugged me before leaving me in my packing and my racing thoughts.

"I returned to Dublin as lost as ever. I studied as hard as I could, but a piece of me always wondered what happened to Sarah. Did she make it to town okay? Back to Galway? But the thought that weighed the heaviest on me was if she was thinking of me, too.

"I was headed back to my dorm one day in early November. Outside my door, a woman with dark brown hair sat with her nose buried in a book.

"I walked closer, 'Can I help…' I lost my words when she looked at me. 'Sarah.'

"I wanted to run and scoop her up into my arms. I wanted to spin her around and kiss her so fiercely she'd never forget my lips.

"I knew I couldn't just do that, so instead I asked, 'How did you find me?'

"Her pale cheeks flushed. 'Some digging. Killorglin is a very small town. Some man named Tiernan, who was up the road from you, was at a pub I called. He took the phone from the barkeeper and gave me your parents' number, and well…' She looked uncertain but finally stood. All my thoughts changed from being excited to see her to shock when I noticed a small swell. My life would never be the same.

"I swallowed. 'Do my parents...' I didn't know how to finish the sentence.

"She shook her head. 'No. I just said we'd met at Puck Fair, and I was looking to reconnect. I didn't feel it was my place if...' She lost her words, and I was sure she wondered how I felt.

"I gestured to the door behind her. 'Let's go in here.'

"I opened the door to my room. Once we were alone, I warred with what I wanted to do next. I still wanted to kiss her, but we had bigger, more important things to sort.

"'I guess you can see I'm...' her words trailed off, her eyes searching. 'Based on the due date, I'd say it's yours. Also, because you were the only person I'd had sex with since last semester.' She shook her head. 'You don't need to know about my sexual history.'

"She pressed her hands to her face, clearly struggling with the conversation. I pulled them down and looked into her beautiful blue eyes.

"'I kind of knew this was a possibility,' I admitted.

"Her mouth dropped. 'How?'"

"My insides twisted. 'I found one of the condoms on the floor broken. You were gone and...' I felt like such an asshole. I should've gone to town. Even if she never wanted to see me again, I should've tried harder to find her. 'I'm so sorry.'

"'I am too. I shouldn't have snuck out.' She licked her lips. 'I didn't want it to be a one-night thing from the moment we kissed, but I didn't want to put pressure on what was supposed to be a little fun at a party.'

"I hesitantly held my hand over her belly. With a smile, she pressed it against the small bump. Tears pricked my eyes. 'We're having a baby?'

"She nodded. 'I only wanted to tell you in case you wanted to be involved and—" I cut off her words with a kiss.

"When we pulled apart, she looked at me hopefully. 'So, you want to be involved?'

"I kissed her again.

"'I really need an answer in words," she whispered, tears filling her eyes.

"'We'll figure it out," I said firmly, "together.'"

Sarah drains the rest of her wine and smiles at the end of the story.

She looks at me with the pale blue eyes that captivated me that night. "We definitely figured it out."

I nod. "And then some."

She laughs, then leans in and kisses me. I've never grown tired of her velvety lips against mine. If anything, I crave them more now than I did when we were younger.

"Twenty years," she says with a chuckle. "Twenty Valentine's Days."

"I wouldn't want to share them with anyone else." I took her hand and kissed her knuckles. "That story makes me think, though."

Sarah tilts her head. "Think about what?"

I stand and walk over to the china cabinet where I hid her gift a month ago. I pull out a jeweled heart-shaped box and set it in front of her.

"I thought we weren't exchanging gifts this year." She looks disappointed.

I tuck some hair behind her ear. "This isn't a gift. This is me righting a wrong from many years ago." I pull a key from my pocket and hand it to her. "You'll need this to open it."

Sarah eyes me suspiciously as she takes the key. She sticks it into the lock on the front of the case and turns it, then slowly opens the lid. She gasps when she sees the one-karat solitaire princess cut diamond ring inside. She looks down at her finger, which has a simple wedding band. It's all we had money for when we got married.

"Connor!"

I get down on one knee and hold the ring out to her.

Tears fill her eyes.

We got engaged mere months after she visited me in Dublin,

but I didn't have a ring. I couldn't afford one because I spent my money moving to Galway. I transferred in my last semester and Sean was born shortly after we graduated. Then we spent all our money moving to Killorglin, building our house, and having three more beautiful children.

I take her hand in mine and ask, "Do you still want to do this crazy life with me?"

"Yes." She nods furiously. "Forever."

I slide the ring on her left ring finger. She cups my cheeks and kisses me deeply.

"Happy Valentine's, Connor."

"Happy Valentine's, my perfect Galway girl."

THE END

LAURA MEREDITH IS a biracial writer from northern Canada. Her novels explore love often between people of two different cultures, as she wanted to create the representation she found lacking in media when she was growing up. When not writing, you can find her knitting, learning embroidery, sewing, reading, or just generally getting lost in the boreal forests of her home with her husband, two young children, Blue Heeler and Basset Hound.

THE ANATOMY LESSON

AMELIA S. FLETCHER

Tropes:

- Paranormal romance
- Friends to lovers
- Strangers to lovers
- Idiots in love

Content Warnings: explicit sex scene (featuring multiple partners, oral sex), loss of virginity, blood (vampire bite).

A WEREWOLF and a vampire walk into a bar—sounds like the start of a bad joke, I know.

But that's exactly how this story starts.

It was a night like any other since most of my nights involved serving the patrons at Poppy's Tavern. My grandpa had founded the place almost eighty years earlier, and once I was old enough, closing up on my own became a regular thing. It's not a big deal; the scoundrels in our part of town know not to mess with me or my family, so I'd never felt like I was in any danger working alone.

In a big city like South Point, humans were only about half the population, so we typically had quite a variety of beings visiting Poppy's, including my sweet Victor. Victor was a were-wolf and had been visiting Poppy's almost as long as I'd been working. Every night that I worked on my own, he was there, silently watching. He was charming, kind, and an absolute gentle-man. Alright, maybe Victor was the reason I never had any trou-ble. Him, and the dagger I kept at my hip.

For years, my mother had been convinced he would ask me to marry him, but since I'm almost twenty-seven now and very much unwed, I feel confident saying she was wrong. Victor was just a nice guy in a not-so-nice part of town, and I doubted I would ever get to have some fun in bed with him; it was also a relief on nights when the patrons tried to get handsy. They weren't fond of his not-so-nice side, which, like most werewolves, was protective of the people he deemed 'his'—and my family had become that.

Like every other night, I was set to close the tavern on my own when Victor came in, smiling at me before settling at the bar. Unlike every other night, he came in with a friend. A vampire. Not so unusual since vampires and werewolves get along just fine, but it was still odd to see Vic with anyone else since he usually kept to himself.

"Evening, Vic." I smiled warmly at him and was happy when he returned it with a small smile of his own. "And welcome to

Poppy's," I said to his friend. "Can I get you something to eat..." I hesitated, "Or drink?"

Please don't ask for blood, please, please, please.

The vampire stared up at me with an appraising look in his light blue eyes, then slowly let a smile warm up his pale features. "You must be Annie." I didn't think any creatures but cats could purr, but his smooth voice did just that, melting over me like warm cocoa. He was just as handsome as Victor, though instead of looking physically intimidating, his lean frame and long hair reminded me of a well-bred nobleman, a different sort of intimidating.

"Er. Yeah. That's me." I glanced at Victor, who was blushing and avoiding eye contact.

"Pleasure is all mine." The vampire held out a hand, which was surprisingly warm when I took it, and without missing a beat, he gently pulled my hand closer and kissed the back of it.

"Knock it off, Charlie," Victor growled at his friend. "Annie isn't yours to play with."

Charlie smiled at me, let go of my hand and then turned to Victor, his smile turning into a mischievous smirk. "Not yet. Maybe she'd prefer a vampire lover instead of a werewolf?"

Excuse me? Had I missed something?

Victor's eyes widened. "I'm not—she's not—" he shot a panicked look in my direction. "It's not like that!"

Charlie chuckled, leaned on the table and tilted his head. "So she's unclaimed then?"

"Hey, I'm right here. I'm not a toy."

They stared at each other briefly before both looked up at me again.

"I'm so sorry, Annie. Charlie's being a dick." Victor pleaded. "Just ignore him?"

Charlie was chuckling though. "You certainly are not a toy. You're a delicious—I mean, *delightful* young lady who deserves more respect than I've given. Please accept my apologies."

I smiled at Victor, hoping he understood I didn't blame him

for his friend's behaviour, and then turned back to Charlie. "Just don't get any ideas," I muttered. "Did you want anything?"

Charlie smirked, "Well. Yes. But I don't think you're on the menu." He winked at me, then leaned back while I struggled to respond. I doubt there's a barmaid in the entire world who could say a patron has never propositioned them, but being hit on by a vampire was a first, and it left me feeling flustered. Maybe a little flattered.

"Fuck off, Charlie." Victor was growling on the other side of the table. "I didn't tell you about her, so you could—" he stopped abruptly, his cheeks turning red.

I coughed awkwardly, turning away so I could pour a mug of ale for Vic.

"So. *Are* you without a mate, sweetheart?" Charlie asked when I plunked down an ale for him as well.

"Are you always so nosey?" I asked, making Victor chuckle quietly.

Charlie smirked. "One of my many talents." He leaned forward, studying me for a moment. "I've got plenty more interesting talents, of course." He winked. I hoped he couldn't hear how loud my heart was pounding. Vampires and werewolves both had far better hearing than humans did.

"So, do you?" He prompted after a moment of silence.

"What?"

"Do you have a mate?"

My eyebrows lifted and drew together. "No?"

He chuckled, shaking his head. "I guess you're not a werewolf then?"

I shook my head. "Just a human. Just a boring, no powers, nothing special, human."

"Ah, perhaps that is why he's being so stubborn about it." He glanced at Victor, who was staring into his mug and doing his best to ignore our conversation. Charlie closed his eyes then, smiling as he drew in a breath. "I wouldn't say there's nothing special about you, sweetheart."

He let the air out through his nose, then opened his eyes again so I could see the hint of lust in their depths. "Do you know why he's been a regular at Poppy's for so long?"

I shrugged. "I thought he liked Poppy's famous beef stew. Or maybe he just likes that we're decent folk in a not-so-decent part of town."

Charlie laughed. "Appealing features, that is true. But no. Do you remember when he started coming here?"

I thought back, shrugging as I answered uncertainly. "Four or five years, I guess?"

"Exactly. Just after you started handling closing on your own a few nights a week, Vic's made a point to come in on those nights to ensure you're safe."

"You've never stepped foot in this place, how exactly do you know that?"

Charlie beamed at me. "Well, since Victor has warmed my bed on and off over the years, it was hard to miss when he became... shall we say, distracted?" His fingers tapped his lips thoughtfully. "It took some time to drag it out of him, but it was certainly a surprise when he told me he'd fallen in love."

"Okay, that's enough." Victor finally snapped, starting to stand up.

Charlie didn't turn from me, only smirking as he continued. "You never would have told her."

"Maybe there's a reason for that—maybe I would have told her on my own!" Victor growled.

I slipped away from the counter while they bickered for a few minutes, pulling the shutters on the windows and locking the front door. The other guests had left as they came in, and I was glad I didn't have to shoo anyone out now. This seemed like something that would take my full attention, and I didn't want any random guests wandering in to distract me.

"I think she'd be much more satisfied with a vampire cock!" Charlie was muttering when I returned to the counter.

"Maybe I'd prefer neither of your cocks. Had you thought of

that?" I said, grabbing a clean mug and pouring some ale for myself.

"You don't have a mate, though." Charlie thunked his mug down on the bar. "And we're both better than any human you've considered. I think you should take us both as your lovers for a night—you won't have a reason to consider anyone else afterwards." He smirked, confident and smug.

Victor growled at Charlie, and though he didn't look sorry, the vampire stopped talking. "I'm sorry. Annie, we'll be off. I shouldn't have brought him—"

"Stop that." I thunked my mug down on the countertop and frowned at the werewolf. "You're both making assumptions and forming opinions without once asking what I think."

There was a beat of silence before Charlie spoke. "She isn't wrong." He bowed his head towards me. "Forgive us both. Please, tell us what you want?"

I wasn't quite sure what to say. I'd never been with any man, human, vampire, werewolf or otherwise, so it wasn't as though I had any preconceived ideas of what sex was like—good or bad. It wasn't because I didn't want to have sex, I'd just gotten so used to brushing off the unwanted advances of the men who frequented the bar I wasn't certain how to say yes.

"I—well. I've never—I mean, that is..." I stammered, trailing off as they both patiently waited for my answer.

"Are you a virgin?" Victor finally asked, his voice low and quiet.

I nodded. "Not that I'm saving myself. It's just..." I trailed off. A smile spread across Charlie's face, and he shoved Victor's shoulder.

"Well, I happen to know a certain werewolf who'd adore showing you how pleasurable a cock can feel." He chuckled. "Or maybe you'd prefer a vampire show you instead?"

I twisted my hands in my apron, suddenly feeling awkward. Instead of answering Charlie, I looked at Victor. Before anything else, I needed to know why he had kept his feelings to himself for so long. "Why didn't you ever tell me?" I asked.

He blushed, looking away. "I'm old. You're human. I'm a werewolf. I can barely stand the thought of watching you grow old and die—and then living without you for the rest of my damn life." His voice had dropped to a whisper by the time he was finished. He huffed then. "At least if I never told you, I would never know what I was missing."

"And yet you've tortured yourself coming here every week for years." Charlie stared at the werewolf, who whimpered and nodded. The vampire looked at me again, his expression softening. "But I'll admit, I understand his thought process. Being immortal can have its drawbacks."

Vic snarled quietly, but Charlie shrugged.

"What? Between what you've told me and what I've seen tonight," Charlie tilted his head to the side, considering my appearance, "I'd say she's not like most of the women in this stupid city." He smiled at me, a fang appearing that lent to his mischievous expression, and winked. "You're likely to bite back—you have depth to go with your grace and beauty. What man wouldn't want to be with you?"

"Thanks, I think?" I muttered and slid my hands into my skirt pockets, feeling awkward.

"He's not wrong." I turned to Victor, who was looking at me with his eyes wide. "When I first came into Poppy's, I was drawn to how pretty you are. But over the years, I've stuck around because of who you are on the inside."

"So?" Charlie prompted, dragging his tongue over his lips.

"So?" I repeated. "You...you seriously want me to sleep with one of you? Tonight?"

Charlie raised his eyebrows. "I believe I suggested both of us."

I think my brain had a momentary lack of function then. I'd fantasized about Victor and one or two handsome strangers before. But never more than one lover, and it had all been in my head. With zero experience, I wasn't sure how to handle one of them, never mind both simultaneously. I blinked slowly. "Aren't werewolves, uh, territorial about their mates?"

"Charlie *is* my mate." There was no hesitation in his response. "He makes it seem like a casual romp here and there, but he knows his companionship means more than that to me. And he's the only person I wouldn't object to seeing you with."

Slowly, I looked between Charlie and Victor, who were sharing an affectionate look. Victor hadn't released my hand, so I reached out to take the vampire's. "Well. I've heard some more brazen women speak of having multiple lovers. At once."

Charlie's eyes lit up, while Victor looked surprised by my words. "Please tell me you're suggesting—"

"You aren't actually suggesting—"

I rolled my eyes. "I'm suggesting you both bed me. At the same time."

Charlie was grinning, his fangs fully out. "Yes! Yes. Oh, please."

Victor was much more reserved. "Annie, are you sure? You've never been with any man, you really want—"

I cut him off, tugging him over the bar to silence him with a kiss. And then melted as he growled, wrapping his free hand around the back of my head to deepen the kiss without any further fuss. I wasn't certain about any of this, but Victor had been watching over me for years, and I trusted him. If Charlie was his mate, that had to mean he trusted him, so I decided I could also trust the vampire.

Charlie must have come around the bar because a wet tongue was suddenly dragging up my neck, a sharp fang teasing the edge of my earlobe as the vampire pressed himself against me. "Fuck, she tastes so good, Vic."

Victor pulled away from me, breathing a bit heavier than he had been and watched as Charlie nuzzled against my neck, nipping and licking to make me shudder against him. "No...stop, Charlie. We can't do this here. A bar countertop is no place for your first time, Annie."

Charlie chuckled against my skin but murmured his agreement before gently nicking my ear with one fang. "Where do you sleep, sweetness?"

Their attention was starting to make my head swim, and it took a moment to understand what they asked of me. "Upstairs."

Without warning, Victor had swept me up in his arms, moving faster than I knew was possible and setting me down a moment later on the bed I used in the upstairs loft. He glanced around, curiosity in his eyes. "This is your room?"

"Just on nights when I close. It's not safe to walk home after dark." I followed his eyes, taking in the small space. It was plain, with a cozy bed against one wall, well-used over the years, with a trunk full of spare clothing and blankets on the floor. The window had a heavy white wool curtain, and a thin blue rug was spread across the floor to keep the morning chill away. It wasn't meant to be home, but it was comfortable enough.

"You deserve so much better." Charlie settled on the bed to my left as Victor sank down to my right. "We could give that to you, you know?"

Vic nuzzled against my neck this time, kissing my pulse while Charlie stroked my cheek tenderly. "Why? What if I'm already happy?"

"I think we can make you happier," Victor murmured.

"So happy," Charlie murmured before kissing me just as fiercely as Vic had moments before. It crumbled the last of my uncertainty, and when he pulled away, I started tugging on the laces of his trousers.

It felt like a tiny storm was surrounding me as, one by one, the layers of clothing we all wore were removed and discarded on the floor. Each man took turns kissing me or licking my exposed neck and shoulders. By the time they had fully disrobed me, I don't think they had left any spot on my body untouched. My head was spinning, delirious with the lust they had spurred within me.

Victor and Charlie sat back then, their eyes looking over me as I lay panting on the bedsheets. They were both glorious in their nudity, and I took the time to take them in, just as they were doing to me. Victor was burlier, with thick thighs and biceps that left no doubt about his strength. Hair covered most of his body, which seemed obvious since he was a werewolf, but it didn't hide the muscles that rippled across every part of him. Charlie was pale, without a hint of hair anywhere. His muscles were less pronounced, and he had a leaner, slimmer body than the werewolf. I wanted to touch both of them, to feel the smooth skin and the soft hair under my fingers before getting to grasp the thick cocks that were pointed at me, hard and eager for me. But the way they stared at me left me frozen; the hunger in their eyes was so intense that I wondered if I had made a terrible mistake.

"I understand," Charlie murmured after they had studied me for several silent moments. The tenderness in his tone relaxed me, reminding me I was in no danger. He turned to the werewolf, stroking his cheek with a tender caress. "I understand why you didn't let me meet her before." Victor accepted a soft, affectionate kiss from the vampire. "She's as delicious as you, my darling wolf."

"She's as beautiful as you are, Charlie." Victor turned back to me, stroking his hands over my torso before kissing me again. "Will you let me be your first?" He asked, one finger twirling around the hardened nipple of my right breast.

"What? But you'll take twice as long." Charlie pouted, then turned his attention to me. He stretched out next to me as Vic's hands continued to stroke across my skin. "Won't you let me be your first, sweetness?"

I'm not sure how I decided, as my mind was so addled with lust and desire I could barely think straight, but between moans and gasps, I managed to tell them. "Victor first—he's known me longer." If Charlie complained, my attention was swallowed by a passionate kiss from the wolf and I didn't hear.

When Victor's mouth engulfed my breast again, Charlie tore my underwear from me and spread my legs. I stretched to see what he was doing, but all I saw was his delighted face descending as he knelt on the floor. His fingers danced up my legs, making me squirm as he tickled the sensitive spots of my thighs. "Fuck, Victor. You can smell her, can't you? She smells so good!"

My wolf paused, stopping just long enough to glance at the vampire. "You aren't going to bite her now—" He growled. I could feel the sharp prick of fangs on the soft inside of my thigh, but no pain followed. Charlie licked the spot once, then dragged his nose along my skin with a quiet, content sound rumbling from his chest.

"Just a taste." His tongue was suddenly dragging along my most private place, drawing a cry out of me.

"Ch-Charlie—what are you...oh. That feels...fuck!"

My entire body shuddered as my back arched, and a ripple of pleasurable sensations rolled over me. It had felt amazing when they had played with my breasts, but this—I had nothing to compare it to, but it felt amazing.

"You like that, darling?" The wolf growled in my ear. His voice seemed deeper, rougher. My eyes snapped open when a damp nose nudged my neck. Victor had changed. A large wolf head stared down at me; the rest of his body was still mostly human but was now covered in thick black fur, as opposed to the hair that I had seen earlier.

Victor's large green eyes watched me for a second, maybe to make sure I wouldn't freak out. I had no reason to, though; he was gorgeous like this, and Charlie's fingers sliding into me were too distracting. The vampire had found my sensitive nub and was sucking greedily on it. "He's gonna stretch you," My wolf murmured, kissing my neck.

"What? Why?"

Victor chuckled, the sound deeper and rougher since he had shifted. I could feel his chest vibrating against my arm before he moved, now kneeling beside me. His large hands grasped his hard manhood, giving me a better view of what would soon be inside me. It was long and thick at the base. The head was dark red, where it tapered at the end. It was a stark reminder that he definitely wasn't human. "Oh, oh fuck. Will that even—" My words were cut off as Charlie thrust his fingers deeper, added another finger and then curled them all within me. I screamed as my vision turned white and my body convulsed. When I could focus on something again, my body was tingling all over, shivering with the aftereffects of—whatever Charlie had done.

"What... Oh, by the Gods—what was that?" I gasped, my fingers tangling in the thick fur of my werewolf as he continued to suckle and grope my chest.

"Haven't you ever touched yourself, darling?" Charlie asked, kissing my thigh while he let me have a moment to recover.

"No—no?" I had no idea what he meant.

"Didn't your mother or a girlfriend ever talk to you about the art of self-pleasure?" He purred, continuing to kiss my shivering skin. He hadn't withdrawn his fingers, and while I tried to understand what he meant, he wriggled them within me.

I couldn't form the words, so I shook my head.

"Oh, darling. Well, I suppose this is a good time for an anatomy lesson." He licked me again, then pulled his fingers out despite my protests. "Ah-ah, be a good girl, sweetness. You'll be rewarded, I promise."

I felt the heat on my cheeks but nodded immediately. Everything Charlie had been doing felt too good, as if it was building up to something bigger, and I didn't want to risk losing that feeling so quickly after just discovering it.

"There are many words to describe these parts," Charlie started, slowly pushing his fingers back into me and quickly pulling them out. He ignored my frustrated whine and continued. "The hole is your vagina. These are the labia," He gently massaged the soft folds of skin on either side and then pinched the sensitive nub that made my entire body jerk. "And that is the clitoris." He grinned at me before pushing his fingers into me again. "A man's cock fits in here like a key in a lock. But some keys are bigger than others, and it takes some work to stretch the lock so it will fit." He pulled his fingers apart slightly as he began to thrust them in and out of me. Victor leaned down, engulfing the nub, my clitoris, in his mouth, and I writhed as my body felt like jolts of lightning spread across me.

"Oh! Oh—Gods!"

"No Gods." Charlie chuckled, then slid a third finger into me. "Only we can give you this, Annie. No Gods, no other men." He thrust roughly, making me yelp and whimper. "Just Charlie and Victor. When you scream, you scream our names. No deities."

"Y-yes! Yes, Charlie! Vic—oh!" I couldn't handle it anymore, and I felt like I was going to explode.

"That's it, let go, Annie, come for us," Charlie demanded. "Let go!"

I did as I was told. The world around me went white, my entire body quaking with an intense surge of pleasure as I screamed.

"Such a good girl." Victor was murmuring as the world returned to focus, his damp wolf nose nuzzling against my ear while Charlie stroked my head. Each of them stroked my skin from breast to hip and back again, leaving trails of tingles in their wake.

"Wh-what happened?" I asked, blinking at them, still dazed.

"That, sweetness, is called an orgasm." Charlie smirked, a look of triumph in his eyes. "And you looked so beautiful when you let go."

"You did so well," Victor added. "I'm looking forward to seeing you come like that every night, if you'll let us?"

"She hasn't even taken our cocks yet," Charlie scolded, but he was grinning.

"Do you think you still want to?" Victor asked, looking worried now.

I thought about how Charlie's fingers in me had felt so incredible. I nodded. "I want more." They both looked delighted by my answer. "Victor?" I turned to him, kissing him. "Please?"

"Anything for you." He shuffled down the bed, positioning himself between my legs again. But he didn't ready himself like I expected. Instead, he leaned down, licking over my vagina a few times with his huge, wet wolf tongue. He growled, licking his lips when he straightened up again. This time he grasped his cock, nudging at my entrance with the swollen tip. "I'll go slow. Tell me if it hurts. If you tell me to stop, I will. Okay?"

I nodded. Charlie was moving beside me, so he was kneeling beside my head. He took one of my hands, squeezing gently. "You still want this, Annie?"

I nodded again. Victor stopped. "Words, Annie. Use your words. Be clear about what you want."

"Yes? I still want you—I want your cock, both your cocks. Please!"

Victor grinned and then slowly pushed the head of his huge wolf cock into me. I groaned, gripping Charlie's hand tightly. Victor didn't move again until he felt me relax. Slowly, he eased into me, stretching me as his cock filled me up. It was good that Charlie had stretched me first because as Victor slowly sank into me, the stretch felt like it was burning, but it also felt amazing. The further he went, the more spots he hit inside, places I didn't even know could feel so good, and I bucked under him, my hips flexing upwards to take the last of his length while I moaned. He stayed still then, panting and staring down at me, his hands travelling up and down my thighs while he took in the spot where we were joined.

"Fuck. Fuck, that looks—" My vampire growled, stroking himself as he, too, took the sight in. "Oh, Annie, sweetness. He fits in you so perfectly." Seeing them both hungry for more drove my need higher. I twisted, grasping Charlie's cock. He wouldn't be inside me until Victor was done, so it seemed fair to pleasure him with my hand while he watched the werewolf fuck me. He jerked, looking down in surprise. "Oh...you little minx. Well, I won't say no. Open your mouth."

The vampire was slightly smaller than Victor, so it looked less like a monster cock. I parted my lips, sticking my tongue out to lick the tip. The bead of liquid there tasted salty, but not unpleasant. Charlie's fingers tangled in my hair as Victor slowly pulled out of me, and the vampire's cock was suddenly filling my mouth. I moaned around him and then let out a garbled yelp as Victor pushed back into me faster than the first time.

They were in perfect sync then, as one pulled out, the other pushed in. Back and forth, quickly building up speed with each thrust until I no longer had any sense except that I loved what they were doing. Victor was rubbing my clit, grunting with each thrust into me, forcing my body closer and closer to another divine orgasm while Charlie gripped my hair and fucked my mouth.

As my body felt like it was close to tipping over the edge once again, Victor let out a loud snarl. "Fuck—fuck, she's so tight. I'm so close...Annie!" He pulled out of me, gripping the base of his cock as he started to stroke with his other hand vigorously.

I whined, frustrated that I had been so close, and Charlie pushed me upwards, wrapping his arms around me so I could use him as support. "Patience, sweetness, we aren't done with you yet. Now, be a good girl and open your mouth. He likes seeing his lovers swallow his seed."

I obeyed, and Charlie rewarded me with his fingers. They sank into me as Victor howled, and a spray of warm, sticky seed flew towards me. Most landed in my open mouth, but my face and chest were drenched in the sticky cream. My wolf stared at me, breathing hard, his tongue licking his lips. He was still stroking himself, and the base of his cock had expanded, swelling under his other hand where he squeezed. He grinned after a moment, the expression more vicious looking on his wolf face. "Fuck, Annie. I didn't think I'd ever see you like this, but—wow. You look so gorgeous like this. Covered in my cum."

Charlie dragged a finger through the sticky fluid, twirling it around one of my nipples before bringing it up to my mouth. "Eat up, that's a good girl." He grinned, scooping more of Victor's seed onto his fingers to feed me with it. "No vampire cock until you're all done."

I whined around his fingers, but before I could voice my

complaint, he pulled his fingers out of me. "Ah, you're a good girl, aren't you Annie?"

I nodded immediately. "Yes. Yes, I'm a good girl." He grinned, then leaned across my chest to drag his tongue through the white spunk. Then he kissed me, pushing everything into my mouth. Victor groaned, watching the erotic sight.

"Shit. You both look so beautiful like that." My wolf whispered. "I should have done this years ago."

Charlie chuckled, looking up at the wolf. "We were missing something, my wolf. And now we have her. Don't regret the past. Look forward to the future." He kissed my neck again, moving us both until I was on my hands and knees, pinned against Victor's furry chest as he settled onto the bed under me. Charlie's slender fingers dragged through the dampness between my legs, humming happily before another object pressed against me. His cock.

"Ready for me now?" He asked, leaning across my back to grip my hair.

"Yes! Yes, please. Please, I want more!"

Both men chuckled, and I yelped as I was jerked forward, suddenly impaled on Charlie as he thrust roughly into me. "I won't be as gentle as our wolfy," He murmured, kissing the back of my neck. "And there will be a little blood."

Blood? The thought only lingered for a second. Charlie had been telling the truth; he wasn't gentle at all. He gripped my hair tightly in one fist, held my hip with his other hand and hammered into me. Below me, Victor played with my breasts or licked my neck whenever he could. Between his attention and Charlie's cock pounding into me, I was certain I had left the mortal plane. I had always thought pain during sex wouldn't be pleasurable, but despite Charlie's rough treatment, I was feeling pure bliss. And then the real pain hit me. Charlie's fangs sank into my neck. It wasn't a tiny nick like he had done earlier on my thigh. No, his fangs were deep in my veins, drawing out the blood he had promised. This wasn't just bliss—he'd sent me straight to paradise, filling my head with a euphoria I had never imagined possible. If he hadn't been holding me in place, I would have collapsed then and there. It felt so good. He snarled, hips shuddering with the final hard thrusts as he came, his seed flowing into me. He wrapped his arms around me, pulling me upright without stopping his feed.

"Wow," Victor whispered. When I cracked my eyes open, he watched us, his eyes filled with awe. "I wish I could paint. I'd capture this image so I never forget how beautiful you look. Does it feel good, Annie?"

I couldn't nod since Charlie was still holding me so tightly. But I managed to croak a slight sound of confirmation. Victor grinned, clearly delighted by the sight. "Good. He hasn't been able to climax like that for close to fifty years. Vampires can't handle wolf blood."

The werewolf's grin widened as his gaze lowered, taking in the sight of our joined bodies. "Can you feel that?" He crawled forward, fingers sweeping up my leg where warm liquid was trickling down my inner thighs, leaking out from around the cock that was still deep inside me. "Probably a good thing vampires can't have children this way since he gets such a kick out of filling his lovers up like this."

Victor pressed a finger to my lips, feeding me some of Charlie's cum. It was sweeter than Victor's, and I gobbled it up eagerly as Charlie withdrew his fangs. The vampire slowly lowered us to the bed, and my two lovers cuddled me between them.

"That was," I said, eyes drifting closed. "I don't know how to describe it. It was better than amazing."

Charlie was silent, licking the wound he had created, so Victor spoke instead. "I guess we'll just have to start having more lessons with you." He said with a wink. "Help you with the vocabulary, yeah?"

I felt delirious between them, still dazed by our activities but comfortable and safe between their strong bodies. "I'll happily listen to my vampire and werewolf professors forevermore," I murmured. "Best lesson I've ever attended."

. . .

THE END

122

AMELIA S. FLETCHER is an author of cozy and spicy romance hailing from Vancouver, BC. She likes making people melt for her characters, and you can define that however you like. Her debut series, Foxtail Grove, is a contemporary small town romance set in the Canadian Rockies, and this story is absolutely nothing like any of that. Future works from Amelia will include slightly more unhinged fantasy romance, kind of like this one. You can learn more on her website, https://asfletcherauthor.wixsite.com/asfletcher.

THE COVE

MARRON KAYE

Tropes:

- Contemporary romance
- Age gap
- Small town
- Instalust/attraction

Content Warnings: one explicit sex scene, mention of cheating/divorce.

Author's Note: This short story is a companion to The Llyn Lakes Series but will not spoil any of the novels, should you choose to read them afterward.

AMY

"Please hold on the line, ma'am, we're checking for the nearest automotive locksmith."

I yelp and pull the phone from my ear as the line switches to unnecessarily loud hold music. The sickeningly sweet love song reminds me what day it is, not that I could forget with the insane amount of lovey-dovey cards that littered the hallways after school. It was the stupid heart-shaped card stuck to my boot that actually precipitated the predicament I'm in now. The one where I'm locked out of my car after dark on the coldest night of the year.

I'd just closed up and was inching across the frozen parking lot of Llyn Lakes Elementary, where I started this year as principal, when I'd noticed the stupid thing stuck beneath my foot. Being the newly divorced humbug that I am, I swiftly bent to remove the offending item and lost my footing on the ice in the process. My bag and keys went flying as I attempted to brace my fall. All I could do was watch as those keys arced through the air on a collision course with a nearby sewer grate. Sprawled out on the cold ground, I'd held my breath as they clanked against the metal, then slipped unceremoniously between the bars.

Of course, my school keys were on that same ring. I'd glanced back hopefully at the dark building as I'd collected the spilled contents of my purse, but I already knew I was the last to leave as my colleagues had all hurried home hours earlier, eager to spend the evening with their partners.

The bitter wind that blows in from nearby Hedd Lake seems to have the ability to seep deep into my bones, a phenomenon that I'd conveniently forgotten about during my years away. And for the first time, as I wait, shivering and alone on Valentine's Day, with my hip throbbing in time with my head, I question my decision to move back to Llyn Lakes.

JOE

"Hey Mike, any chance you could stay a little later tonight? Just got a call for a tow but I was hoping to finish up with the brakes on the Honda."

The older man frowns. "Sorry, no can do. The wife'll kill me if I'm home late on V-day."

I grunt in annoyance. *Riiight.* The day of hearts and flowers.

"I'm takin' her dancing," he announces proudly.

"You dance?" I raise my brows, eyeing him in surprise.

He chuckles, running a hand over his protruding belly. "Not well, but I can suck it up once a year." He smiles, his harsh face softening as he thinks of his wife. "She's worth it."

It's not a sentiment I can relate to, having thoroughly enjoyed bachelorhood for much of my adult life.

I could probably hit up the bar and find a townie to do some dancing of my own with, but after being single as long as I have, I've pretty much over-fished that particular lake. There may be plenty of options in the summer months when our town population doubles with tourists, but this time of year it's slim pickings.

And fuck, I'm getting sick of the hook-up life anyway.

Lately, as I've watched my friends all couple off and settle down, I've begun to wonder if maybe I'm missing out. Much as I hate to admit it, I'm lonely. I don't begrudge any of them their happiness, but I'm starting to feel like the dude in that Brian Adams song where the band breaks up. So and so quit...another guy got married. You know the one.

I sigh and wave a hand in his direction. "Better get out of here, then. Don't want to keep her waiting."

He shoots me a grateful smile, already pulling on his jacket.

"Have fun," I call belatedly as the door swings shut behind him.

Guess I'm in for another night alone in front of the TV. After I run out and deal with this roadside assistance call, of course.

Fuckin' Valentine's Day.

AMY

An old tow truck pulls into the lot, the hook and chain rattling noisily against the boom.

Thank God.

Hopping from foot to foot, I wave eagerly as the driver backs up to my front bumper. The door opens and a strong jean-clad leg emerges, followed by a thick Carhartt jacket that does little to disguise the broad shoulders beneath. The man is tall, and even with the glare of the truck's lights, I can tell he's attractive. He slams the door and moves in my direction, eating up the distance with long confident strides.

"Hear we've got some lost keys," he calls, then slows, squinting against the dim light. "Holy shit. Miss Parsons?"

I haven't been called that in a long time. "It's Horton, now," I say. "Have we met?"

"Oh." He ignores my question, asking instead, "Married?"

No idea why I decide to indulge him, this man who seems to know me, but I do. "*Was,*" I reply, then repeat, "Have we met?"

He clears his throat. "I was in your twelfth-grade English class."

Whoa.

"I haven't taught English in years." Or high school, for that matter.

His chuckle is deep and throaty, and I feel it low in my belly. "Well, I haven't been a student in years."

He moves closer and my breath catches as his features sharpen into focus.

Jesus, he's hot.

"Joe Sutton." He offers a gloved hand which I accept. His shake is firm, but not too strong, and I'm surprised when he doesn't immediately release my hand. "It really is you," he murmurs, studying my face with a near-wondrous expression that catches me off guard. If I weren't so frozen right now I'd be blushing.

Wait a minute.

Sutton?

Once more I take in his tall frame, trying to reconcile it with the more youthful, slightly lanky one that I recall. Sliding my gaze over his face I note the pale eyes—blue, I think—and the dark blond hair just peeking out from beneath his hat. The jawline is sharper, and covered with a pale scruff that, coupled with his worn jeans and utilitarian jacket, gives him a deliciously rakish look. He's no longer the boy from my memory, but...

"Joey?"

He nods, clearly pleased that I remember him. For a moment I'm lost to thoughts of the past. One where I was young and full of excitement about the future. One where Joe was...even younger. I'm surprised, when I shake off the memories, to find him still holding my hand—and standing awfully close. I have to crane my neck to meet his eyes, eyes that stare down at me with...*heat?*

I drop his hand and take a jerky step back, shocked by the answering flush that spreads through my body despite the chill air.

He clears his throat. "Well, let's get this hooked up and back to the shop." He gestures to his truck. "Hop in and warm up."

☙

"Surprised you remember me," Joe says a few minutes later while pulling out onto the street.

"How could I forget?" I chuckle. "You were a constant disruption."

He runs a hand over the stubble on his chin, the raspy sound eliciting a shiver from me that has nothing to do with the cold. "Sorry about that."

"When you even attended class," I add.

He shoots me a sheepish look. "Wasn't much of a reader back then."

"But you are now?" I ask curiously.

"Got two friends that work at the library." He shrugs. "One of 'em put me on to thrillers."

I sit up a little straighter at this. "I love thrillers."

"Yeah?" He pulls his eyes from the road, turning to me with a wide grin and somehow looking even more attractive. I shouldn't be thinking about that. He's a former student after all. But...that was a long time ago. He's certainly all *man* now.

"Mm-hmm," I murmur, suddenly speechless.

He returns his attention to the road and I take the opportunity to study his profile. Strong brow, straight nose, soft, almost pouty lips. Really kissable lips.

I squirm a little in my seat as tension starts to twist low in my belly.

"You like Sandy Dillon?"

I've never had such a visceral reaction to a man before, but, this is silly. He's got to be a decade younger than me. I need to snap out of this, whatever *this* is. He might be the hottest man I've ever seen in real life, but that was definitely not heat I saw in his eyes.

I'm tired and it was dark.

I'm still busy chastising myself when I realize he asked me something.

"Huh?" I ask, then immediately cringe—that's how fifteen years in education stacks up against hormones.

"The writer," he prompts, and if I'm not mistaken, he's smirking. My face flushes and I panic that he might be able to read my thoughts.

"Oh, uhm, yeah, I've read a few of his, but nothing recent," I manage to get out.

"I just finished his latest. Lots of twists. You should check it out."

"I will," I murmur, still struck by his ridiculous good looks and my even more ridiculous reaction to him.

"You alright?" he asks, as we near the turn-off to the garage.

"Fine," I say, feeling utterly embarrassed, even if he has no clue what his presence is doing to me.

We stop at a red light and he shifts once again to study me. "You sure? You seem a little...flustered."

Crap. Maybe he *can* read my thoughts.

Or maybe I'm just that obvious. That *pathetic*.

"I'm fine," I repeat, this time with more conviction.

"Okay." The light changes and he pulls through the intersection. I peek over at him as we turn into the shop's lot, watching as his lips tip up into a smirk once more. "I was a shitty student," he says. "Always was better with my hands. You commented on my poor attendance earlier, but the funny thing is, I went to your class more than any others. Wanna know why?"

He throws the truck into park and faces me. In the light from the building, I can see that his eyes are indeed blue, and they're taking me in with an intensity that steals my breath. Unable to look away, I stare back at him, watching as they appear to darken.

"Why?" I whisper.

"Cause I had the biggest fucking crush on you, Miss Parsons," he says, then slips from the truck with a wink.

The door slamming behind him rattles me to my core.

❧

"So Miss Pars—" he shakes his head. "Mrs. Hort—" he tries again but cuts himself off, unsure what to call me.

It's twenty minutes later and I've had some time to collect myself while he worked to unhitch my car then disappeared into a back room.

"Amy," I offer as he approaches me now. And there's that smile again, the one that lights up his stupidly handsome face. He nods, locking eyes with mine, and if I'm not mistaken, his grin turns a little wolfish.

No. Nope. Not going there again. Even though he said he had a crush on me. Had, I remind myself. He *had* a crush on me.

"I've got good news and bad news."

"Oh. What's the good news?"

"Re-keying this will be a piece of cake."

"Okay, good. That's good."

"No spares?"

I shake my head. "Lost in the move. So...what's the bad news?

"I'll need to order a new fob and ignition lock cylinder. Won't be able to get 'em in til Monday."

"That's alright. I don't have much planned for this weekend."

"I can give you a ride home."

"That's not necessary, I'll call a cab."

The scent of soap washes over me and once again I'm surprised at how close he suddenly is. "I'm driving you," he murmurs, then reaches out and tucks a loose strand of hair behind my ear. His hand lingers, thumb ghosting over my jaw and I bite my lip. He hums, a noise that rumbles up from deep in his throat, and his gaze—his most definitely heated gaze, there can be no doubt now—zeroes in on my lips.

"Fuck me," he groans. "Those lips ..." and I lean in, dying to hear what it is about my lips, but he shakes his head, abruptly stepping back and holding something out between us.

Disappointment sweeps through me and I look down to find...a book?

"What's this?" I manage to get out amid my confusion.

I thought—

Well, it doesn't matter.

"*A Fractured Vow*."

I raise an eyebrow in question.

"The Sandy Dillon book? Thought I might've left it here and I was right. Keep it."

"Oh, no, I couldn't."

"Borrow it, then."

"Borrow it," I repeat.

"That way I have an excuse to see you again."

My heart rate kicks up at his words.

"You'll see me next week when I pick up my car."

He makes a show of looking me up and down. I've never been thin, but when I was younger I was better able to embrace my curves. Since discovering that my husband was cheating on me, though, I've done my fair share of comfort eating. That, coupled with the stress of the divorce, relocation, and a new higher-pressure job has resulted in those curves being thicker than ever. These days I struggle with feeling attractive, let alone sexy, but the way this man is looking at me...

Holy hell.

"Thinkin' that might not be enough," he says, then throws me another one of those winks. "Now come on, gorgeous, let's get you home."

JOE

Miss. Parsons.

She was my dream woman at seventeen and, fuck me, nothing's changed. She's still the sexiest thing I've ever seen. Long silky red hair—and the real kind, not from a bottle. She even smells like I remember, that delicious fruity scent that used to linger in her classroom. It has me in a goddamn chokehold sitting this close to her in my truck.

"So, no Valentine's date tonight?"

She scoffs as I pull onto her street. "Nope."

"Why do you say it like that? I figure you'd have men lining up to take you out."

She blushes. Again. She's been doing a lot of that tonight and it has my dick twitching in my pants. The look she gives me, though, is one of disbelief, and I can't imagine why. Does she not know how stunning she is? How...fuckable? Those curves...just, damn.

"Guess I'm a little anti-love since my divorce," she says with a shrug, and it's hard to believe any man could have let her go. "Valentine's Day is just..." she trails off.

I wait to see if she'll say more, but she doesn't, keeping her gaze averted as she stares out the window.

"Sorry to hear that. I get it, though. Seems like everyone around me is busy celebrating their relationships tonight and I'm just getting ready to binge-watch *Case Closed*. Alone."

She snorts and it's freaking adorable. "That's my plan too."

"No shit. You like true crime?"

She hums and the sound goes straight to my dick. "Love it."

"Me too! Though I can't ever find anyone to watch with me. My buddies are all cops, and they say it hits too close to home. Guess I can understand why they wouldn't want to see that stuff in their down time."

"Makes sense. I have a realtor friend who complains that every city has its own house-hunting show now, and she hates it."

I chuckle.

She signals for me to pull over and I stop in front of the second-to-last house on the street. The homes here are set farther apart and the cute little bungalow surrounded by trees feels more isolated than I'd expect for this part of town. Still, it manages to look welcoming all lit up with landscape lighting that sparkles against the snow.

I kill the ignition and turn to face her, reluctant to see her go. She squirms under my gaze and I have to fight the urge to pull her into my lap.

"You gonna be able to get in?" I ask, it only just occurring to me that she likely lost all of her keys down that sewer.

She nods, tucking a strand of hair behind her ear. "I have a keypad on the door."

"Good." My voice sounds husky even to my own ears. Fuck, I want her.

"Well..." she says, then stops, clearly casting around for something else to say to prolong this moment, this night.

She's feeling this too.

"Well," I repeat, and her eyes meet mine. The spark from earlier is still there, but see indecision too. She bites her plump bottom lip, and all I can think about is how badly I want to feel that mouth wrapped around my cock.

I decide to help us both out.

"You thinkin' about inviting me in to Netflix and chill, gorgeous?" The smirk I shoot her way is pure sex, but I lighten it by bouncing my eyebrows suggestively. It serves to break the tension, but also to let her know in no uncertain terms that I'm interested.

She sucks in a sharp breath and I hold one of my own, desperate for an answer but also worried that I've overstepped. She's an intriguing mix of sexy yet insecure, somehow, but when she huffs out a laugh, I'm glad I asked.

"The Netflix part, anyway," she says with an answering smirk that tells me everything.

Fuck yeah, this is happening.

"*Case Closed*?" I ask, and we both know we won't be watching anything.

She licks her lips and nods again, meeting my eyes. "*Case Closed.*"

AMY

We're barely through the door when he's on me, shoving me up against the wall. When his mouth descends on mine, it's with fervour, the need pouring off of him in waves. He nips at my bottom lip and I open for him, his tongue sweeping in to tangle with mine. I meet his urgency with an avidness of my own, sliding my hands up his firm chest and around his neck to tangle in the curls peeking out from his toque. In a moment I have it off and discarded somewhere behind him, my fingers pulling and fisting in his thick locks. He groans into my mouth, the evidence of his arousal pressing hard and demanding against my belly as he pins me with his hips.

I whimper at how good this feels, how wound up I am.

I can't believe I'm doing this but...it feels right.

I need it. Need *him*.

I haven't been with anyone since my ex, and he did very little in the final years of our marriage to make me feel attractive or wanted. This man acts like he wants to devour me, though, and even with the number that's been done on my self-confidence, I believe him.

Joe's hands are everywhere, squeezing my hips, cupping my breasts. I don't even remember him removing my jacket, but there it is, pinned and hanging between me and the wall. He breaks the kiss, moving to my jaw, licking and sucking beneath my ear before biting down on my lobe and tugging gently.

"You want this?" he asks against the skin of my neck and I nod, but he pulls back to study my face. "Need the words," he says firmly.

"Yes," I gasp. "Yes, I want this." I meet his eyes. "You."

"Thank fuck," he murmurs, then slides his hands around to grip my ass. When I realize what he's intending to do, I shake my head, pressing against his chest to stop him.

This is too embarrassing.

Again I feel his attention on my face, which burns even hotter than before, and I hope he interprets the deepened flush as one solely of arousal. Somehow, though, I know he's reading more than I want him to.

I know he's going to force me to say it.

"I'm too heavy," I whisper, unable to meet his eyes.

"Nonsense. You're perfect," he says, and his voice is full of conviction. He swats my ass. "Now hop up, Miss Parsons, and show me the way to your bedroom."

With that, he lifts me.

It seems effortless, so I do as he says. I shove my insecurities down deep and wrap my legs around his hips. Gripping onto his shoulders, I bury my face in his neck allowing the clean and manly scent of him to soothe my nerves.

"End of the hall on the left."

JOE

I throw her down on the bed and rip off my coat. She seems as desperate as I am, quickly unbuttoning her blouse while I pull my shirt over my head. When the silky fabric falls away and her tits are revealed, round and full and barely contained by her white lacy bra, I—

I just stare at her.

Sprawled out across the mattress, her hair wild and silvered by the moonlight coming in through the window. Her lips are dark and swollen from my kisses. She's propped up on her elbows, chest heaving with panting breaths, and gazing up at me through thick-lashed bedroom eyes.

'Come fuck me' eyes.

"Joe?" she whispers, breaking me out of my trance.

"Jesus," I breathe. "I think you short-circuited my brain."

Even in the low light, I see when she blushes, and I watch in wonder as the flush spreads down her neck and across her cleavage. I lick my lips wanting nothing more than to chase it with my tongue. Moving in to kneel beside her on the bed, I lock eyes with hers in question. She nods, and I reach behind to unclasp her bra. The fabric falls away and her fuckin' glorious tits spring free, full and creamy, and tipped with the prettiest little nipples. They're peaked and begging for my mouth, but first...

I reach around to the bedside, fumbling for the lamp switch.

"What are you doing?" She sounds alarmed.

"Need to see you in more than just moonlight, gorgeous. Want to know if those sweet nipples are as rosy pink as your mouth."

She bites her lip, looking nervous, and I realize she's feeling self-conscious about her body again. Her full-figured, dangerously curved, incredible body.

"I promise you, sweetheart, there's not one thing about you that doesn't turn me on and take my breath away, and puttin' on a light won't change that. On second thought," I grin, "that much visual stimulation just might stop my heart."

She giggles and I take it as permission to switch on the light, my gaze roving greedily over her exposed skin. She watches me, and I hope she can see the reverence in my eyes.

She's soft.

Sensual.

Irresistible.

I pounce, covering her body with mine, and she giggles again, her worries, her inhibitions, effectively banished. And when I close my mouth over one hardened nipple, that adorable sound turns into a soft moan. She writhes beneath me, desperate for more, so I press my groin into hers, grinding my aching cock against her core through our clothes. I move to her other breast, needing to be sure I worship both properly. I lick in teasing circles, increasing her squirming until she interrupts me with a groan.

"Joe," she whines, and I put her out of her misery, sucking the turgid peak into my mouth.

"Ohhh, God!" she cries out, bucking against me, and I know it's time.

Moving back to kneel beside her, I unzip her pants and yank them down, taking her underwear along with them. She lifts her hips to help me then lets her legs fall open, exposing her glistening pussy to my greedy sight. I chuckle at her wantonness, pleased that she's so clearly ready for me. Sliding a finger through her wetness, I growl in approval when it slips easily between her soft folds.

"This all for me, gorgeous?" My voice is thick with lust, barely recognizable even to myself. I don't think I've ever been this hard for someone. Not since I was a teenager anyway, and well...that tracks.

I can't believe I'm about to fuck Miss Parsons.

Gathering her slickness, I bring it up to circle against her clit, enjoying the way she moves with me, chasing the pressure. The whimpers of pleasure, of need, that fall from her lips only serve to increase my own desperation for her as I slide my hand back down and thrust a finger inside.

"Yes," she calls out, "more."

I oblige, giving her a second, and then a third, stretching her, preparing her for what comes next. I pump my fingers into her again and again, scissoring and twisting, watching with awe as the tension builds, as her eyes squeeze shut and her hips rise in time with my movements. When I curl my fingers against that bundle of nerves that I know will set her off, she does just that—crying out as she pulses around me and flooding my hand with her juices. I study her every micro-expression as she rides the waves of her orgasm, her head thrown back against the mattress, body awash in bliss.

She'd already been the most beautiful woman I've ever seen, but Miss Parsons in the throes of passion is something else.

I shake my head in awe when she opens her eyes, her gaze slowly finding mine. I hold her stare as I raise my hand to my lips and suck my fingers into my mouth. She watches, wide-eyed, while I lick her arousal from my fingers.

"Been desperate to taste you," I murmur. "But if I eat you right now I'm gonna come. This'll hold me over until round two."

"Round two?"

"Better believe it," I assure her, and back off the bed to finally discard my jeans and grab a condom from my wallet. I leave my briefs on, wanting her to do the honours. She sits up and comes to the edge of the bed, watching me in anticipation as I move back to stand between her legs.

"Take me out, angel," I order, and she eagerly does as she's told, reaching into my underwear and gripping my shaft in her delicate hand. She gives me a squeeze before pulling me out, releasing my cock to bob free and proud against my belly as she shoves my briefs down my legs. Pure male satisfaction washes through me as she takes in my size. When she meets my gaze, though, there's no trepidation there, only resolve, and a slow-spreading grin.

"Lie back," I tell her, and she again follows my direction. I fold her legs back against her body, opening her up wider for me, and instruct her to hold onto her knees. "Gonna need to bury myself as deep as possible, Miss Parsons, so you make sure to hold on tight, okay?" I remain standing, with her bent in two at the edge of the bed. Her tits are shoved together between her knees, her sweet pink pussy dripping down over her puckered hole and onto the bedding, and it's the most erotic thing I think I've ever seen.

"Just fuck me, Joe. *Please*," she begs, and the desperation in her voice spurs me to action. I move in close and run my throbbing dick between her soaked folds, torturing us both with the sensation before finally rolling on the condom. She groans, watching me, and I tap the head against her clit eliciting more delicious sounds from her. I line myself up, pausing to meet her eyes, then push in. I do it fast, taking her in one firm stroke, the both of us groaning in unison at the penetration. She's hot, and tighter than I've ever fucking felt, and my heart stutters at the feeling of her enveloping me. Stretching for me. Molding to me.

She's mine.

Fuck me, but she's *mine*.

The thought should scare me, but it doesn't. She's been my fantasy since I was seventeen—one that's managed to linger all these years—and goddammit, the reality is so much better. So much more.

She's sexy as fuck, but she's also sweet, cute, and smart, and our conversation revealed we have more in common than I would have expected. She's a complex mix of confident and shy, and I find that so incredibly endearing while also taking it as a personal challenge. It's my duty to erase all doubts about her body from her mind.

She's a dream come true, and I want her for more than just one night.

I want her for every night.

"Move," she pleads, and I do, pulling almost all the way out, before thrusting in again to the hilt. She whines, and I do it again, savouring the drag and pull, the friction of our bodies moving together. I quickly find my rhythm, setting a steady pace as I build us up. Tension coils at the base of my spine and I worry that I won't last long. I crawl onto the bed, leaning over her, needing to be closer, needing to get even deeper. This angle allows me to rub my pubic bone against her clit with each thrust. She lets go of her legs on a whimper, dropping them to wrap around my hips as she pulls me in for a frantic kiss. It's wild and sloppy. Fucking perfect. I thrust my tongue into her mouth, mirroring the way I continue to fuck into her swollen pussy. She reaches between us to caress my balls. The soft touch is a jarring contrast to the force and depth of my pistoning hips and I break our kiss, panting against her neck at the feeling.

My cock is painfully hard, and I know I'm almost there.

"Need you to come with me now, gorgeous," I grunt, then grind against her clit on the next thrust.

"Yes," she cries out, and I do it again. She plants her heels on the mattress and rears her hips, meeting me thrust for thrust, chasing her climax.

"Yes!" she repeats, and then her muscles clamp down around me, clenching and pulsing her release as she rockets into oblivion. I'm moments behind, stilling as my cock starts kicking furiously inside her. She's squeezing me so good as I throw my head back and groan, shooting my load into the condom, imagining one day taking her bare and painting her insides with my cum.

White lights dance behind my eyes and I release the breath I'd been holding as I drop down on top of her, managing only at the last moment to catch myself on my elbows. She wraps her arms around me as my face comes to rest in the valley of her breasts.

"Wow," she breathes, and I nod, smiling against her chest, understanding now what my friends meant when they called their women game-changers.

THE SOUND of a door closing startles me awake and I shoot up to a sitting position, rubbing my face and blinking blearily as I take in my surroundings.

A grin spreads across my face as the night before comes rushing back to me, and my heart does a little stutter in my chest at the memory. We'd stayed up half the night talking—about anything and everything—then I'd licked her til she screamed before falling into the deepest sleep I've had in years. I'm disappointed not to be waking up next to her, but dropping a hand to the mattress and feeling the lingering warmth from where she'd lain tells me she hasn't been gone long.

Anxious to find her, I climb from the bed, dressing quickly, and making my way down the hall. Moving into the kitchen gives me an idea of where she may have gone. Sliding glass doors in the small breakfast area lead to a patio and the footprints in the snow look recent. Deciding that maybe she needs a little space, I set the coffee maker to brew then retrace my steps to the bedroom and through to the attached bath where I clean up, stealing some mouthwash in anticipation of locking lips again soon.

Returning to the kitchen, I search through her cupboards for mugs and pour the coffee, then retrieve my boots and put them on at the back door. Following her footsteps, I trek across the yard to a copse of trees. The mild sun peeks through the canopy as I find the narrow path, which eventually opens into a small cove. Packed snow covers the area where the ice meets the shore indicating frequent visits.

She stands at the lake's edge with her back to me, her breath visible in the chill morning air. I watch her shoulders rise as she draws in a deep lungful, expelling it slowly before turning to face me.

AMY

"You're still here."

Is it possible that he's gotten even more handsome in the minutes since I left him in bed? His hair is mussed from all the pulling I did on it last night, and the memory makes me breathless.

"Yep."

"And...you made me coffee?"

He nods, striding over to join me and holding out a mug.

I accept it with a timid smile. "Thanks."

He nods again, studying my face, and I turn to look out over the lake once more. He follows suit, sipping his coffee quietly as the sun rises higher in the sky.

"It's beautiful out here," he says finally.

"Mm-hmm."

"I had no idea this was even a waterfront property," he murmurs taking in the sheltered little inlet.

"Technically. I've thought about clearing away some of the trees to have a view of the lake from my patio, but there's just something about taking the hidden path to this secret little spot. It's so peaceful, you know? When I break through the woods and catch that first glimmer of light reflected on the water it just... makes me feel like I'm the only person in the world, I guess."

"Yeah," he agrees and I know he can feel it too, how special this place is. "You come out here a lot, then?"

"When I need to think."

"Or...to hide?" he asks. And I hear the slight note of accusation in his tone.

I sigh and turn to him.

"I was giving you time to leave without making it awkward," I admit.

He swallows, and I watch his Adam's apple bob in his throat. "Do you want me to leave?"

"No?" I whisper, but it sounds like a question.

"You sure about that?"

"I just—" I shrug, embarrassed.

"What?"

I shake my head.

He steps further into my space and, with a finger under my chin, forces me to meet his eyes.

"You just what?" I bite my lip, wanting to turn away, but his intense blue eyes hold me in place. "Amy."

I think that's the first time he's said my given name, and it scares me how much I love the sound from his lips.

"I just figured this was a one-off. Some kind of..." I pause, searching for the right words.

He raises his eyebrows, but stays silent, allowing me to collect my thoughts.

I sigh, then shrug. "Some kind of re-living of your youth, I guess. Finally realizing a high school dream and banging the old crush out of your system."

He studies me for a long moment, eyes roving over my face.

"I won't deny that the thought kept going through my head last night: 'I can't believe I'm kissing Miss Parsons'...'I can't believe I'm touching Miss Parsons'...'I can't believe I'm fucking Miss Parsons.'" He chuckles, and the sound goes straight to my core. "And let me tell you, *Miss Parsons*, it was everything my seventeen-year-old self could have imagined and more." A slow and cheeky grin spreads across his face, and I can't help but smile too, though my cheeks are burning at his words. Eventually, though, his smile drops, his expression turning serious. "But this is no one-off for me, Amy."

My heart skips. It's super hot when he calls me Miss Parsons, but hearing him call me Amy again just does something to me.

Still, this can't be real.

"I like you," he continues. "I want to spend more time with you. Get to know you better."

"But you're...so young."

He scoffs. "Hardly."

"Okaaay, then, I'm so *old*."

He grabs my chin again in his hand. "Don't fucking say that about my girl."

"Your girl?" I rear back, voice squeaking in surprise.

"Maybe I'm getting a little ahead of myself," he hedges with a cocky half-smile, then shrugs, his features again turning serious. "I can see it, though, can't you? We're good together." He gestures between us. "There's something here. I know you feel it too."

"We had one night," I counter.

"And tonight will be two. That is if you let me stay. Then, maybe on night three, I could take you out?"

"You want to take me out," I repeat, my voice dripping with disbelief, but he just nods. I search his eyes but find only sincerity there. Sincerity, and something else. Hope.

"You don't mind being seen with a woman who's a decade your senior?"

"What did I say about speaking 'bout my girl like that?" he growls.

Again, I search his face, but...he does appear to mean what he says.

Slowly, I smile.

His responding grin causes my heart to soar.

We're doing this.

He takes my mug and sets them both down in the snow before pulling me in close and claiming my mouth. That's exactly what it is—a claiming. And we remain there together, embracing in my tiny cove until the sun is high overhead.

Joe drops me off at school on Monday morning and is there waiting for me with my car when classes let out. As I pick my way —more carefully this time—across the icy lot toward him, he grins and holds up a new set of keys.

"Hey, gorgeous," he greets me, planting a soft kiss on my lips. "How was your day?"

"Good. Even better now. How was yours?"

"Got your new lock installed."

"I see that. Thanks."

"Welcome." He smiles. "So...whatcha got planned for tonight?"

"Don't know," I shoot him a coy smile. "Was thinking of maybe watching some *Case Closed*."

Later that night, when he sinks inside me...when I writhe beneath him...when he holds me close and whispers against my skin that I'm his everything, I can't help but be grateful for the events that brought us here.

Together.

And we owe it all to a lost key and a new lock.

THE END

MARRON KAYE WROTE her first novel at the age of forty, proving that it's never too late to chase your dreams. A long-time lover of soap operas and romantic fiction, she credits her grandmother with introducing her to the genre. She lives in Toronto, Canada, with her dog, Rowan, and her turtle, Franklin. The geography of Llyn Lakes, her debut series, is inspired by a town near her family's cottage—a place she lovingly calls her forever happy place. You can learn more at her website, MarronKaye.com.

KNEADING LOVE

HEATHER GREY

Tropes:

- Contemporary romance
- Strangers to lovers
- Forced proximity
- Instalove

Content Warnings: one explicit sex scene, mention of claustrophobic space.

Author's Note: This short story is set in an existing series. Both characters are present in the *Bluefield Beach* series, and have appeared as side characters in the series.

DIANA

"I'll be fine"

"No, go and enjoy yourselves"

"I can handle it"

"You should turn off your phone, really disconnect"

"It will be great"

Spoiler alert, it could be better. It is very *very* cold. I mean it's February in Ontario so cold is to be expected but typically that happens outside, and I'm not currently outside. No, I am very much inside the walk-in fridge at the café I work at.

There's a storm raging outside so at least I'm not out there, right?

The frozen butter and scones can at least keep me company. *When has butter ever steered me wrong?*

When Liana, the owner of the café, mentioned wanting to take a trip with her husband for their wedding anniversary, I was quick to offer my services here at the café. I'm sure getting away for Valentine's Day or any holiday involving sweets can't be easy when you earn your living selling them, so I thought this was the perfect opportunity for me to step up and show my appreciation to Liana for the job and creative freedom she has offered me here.

I love my job.

I love trying new recipes, leaning into seasonal favourites, and creating food that brings people together.

Cookie dough is now officially off that list.

Cookie dough is what I was looking for that led me to be locked in the walk-in freezer, alone on Valentine's Day. It's on my shit list now.

It's not like I have someone to celebrate today with. No, of course not. I have terrible taste in men. Bad. Atrocious. I can't trust my taste in men. So being alone on Valentine's Day is fine with me. I just wish I wore a thicker sweater.

It's only negative three, so I've been colder with fewer clothes. In university, I would stand in line for the bar in a tiny dress with no jacket to avoid paying for coat check. I had alcohol to warm me up then, but I'll survive this. No one dies in a freezer, I think. It's not something I've ever researched. Maybe I should have?

Now, on one of our busiest days of the year, you would think this place would be bustling with customers and other staff but of course, that isn't the case. No, snowmageddon hit about thirty minutes after I arrived and I don't think anyone can see more than a couple of feet in front of them, let alone drive here for all their preordered baked goods. The whole town is hiding in their homes, warm.

What a bunch of assholes.

So, I will be sitting here, without my phone, snacking on raw cookie dough until someone braves the snow-covered roads and sidewalks and discovers I'm in here.

&

JUST AS I finish my third game of tic-tac-toe against myself on the frosted wall, I hear heavy footsteps from somewhere in the café. I immediately get to my feet and bang my cold fists against the door.

"HELP! I'm back here! I'm stuck in the freezer!"

A mumbled voice responds but I can't make out who it is or what they've said. The footsteps grow closer before the voice grows clear.

"Is someone back here?" A deep voice asks.

"Yes!" I practically scream. "I'm locked in the freezer. Can you open the door?"

"Shit. Okay give me a second," they respond. The door rattles and so does my body. The anticipation of getting out of here and into the warm is so great I almost miss the next words out of their mouth. "Does this thing even lock? Is there a key? How did you get locked in here?"

"It doesn't lock..." I trail off as realization hits me. I was so preoccupied thinking about being locked in here that I didn't think about the logistics of the situation. Of course, there isn't a lock on the walk-in freezer. People would get stuck in here all the time if it did. That's a safety risk. But if I'm not locked in, why isn't the door opening?

"Um, miss..."

"Diana," I say. "My name is Diana."

"I wish we were meeting under different circumstances, Diana. My name is Henri. How did you get stuck in there?"

Henri? I don't know a Henri and in a town as small as Bluefield, that is fairly unusual, especially in the winter. We get an influx of tourists in the warmer months but I can't imagine why anyone would want to visit here this time of year.

I'm distracted from my wandering thoughts when Henri says, "Diana? Are you okay?"

Right. He asked me a question and instead of answering, I had a conversation with myself in my head.

"Sorry! Yes, I'm okay, I guess. I don't know how I'm locked in here. The door closed behind me which it always does, but then never opened. I don't know what's wrong."

"Is there someone we should call for help?"

"The fire department? I don't know. I don't have my phone with me but no one is going to be quick to get here with this storm. What were you doing out in this weather?"

"One second," he says before I hear the sound of footsteps fade away.

I hope he comes back. He has a nice voice. It's soothing. If I'm going to be stuck here for the foreseeable future, it would be nice to have some company.

Suddenly his voice is back. "Okay, I called for help but you were right. There's a bunch of accidents in the area so the operator said it would be a couple of hours. How cold are you? What are you wearing?"

I wish that line was said while I had on something sexy and not an old black sweater, yoga pants, an apron, and sneakers. It's probably a good thing Henri can't see me. I'm not stopping traffic with my current outfit.

"I have a sweater on and pants. It's not the most comfortable outfit but it's manageable with the temperature, I think."

"I wish I had something I could use to break this door down but I don't. I'm sorry."

"Don't apologize," I insist. "This is some sort of freak accident and when I get out of here, I will be propping this door open from now on!"

"That sounds like a smart plan," Henri agrees. "So, to answer your earlier question, I just got into town yesterday. My father is moving into the new retirement home in town. I had dinner with him there last night and figured I would get some food today to stock up the fridge at the rental I'm staying in for the month while my dad settles. I woke up to the storm but my options were to bundle up and get something to eat or starve. I chose to trudge through the snow and that brought me here. No other stores on Main Street had their lights on so I could hardly see anything. The place was like a beacon of light guiding me in. I'm not glad you're stuck in there but I'm glad I made the choice to go out in the snow and found you."

HENRI

"I'm glad I made the choice to go out in the snow and found you."

Did that really just come out of my mouth? Have I completely lost it? This poor woman is freezing, literally freezing inside a freezer. One that I don't know how to get her out of and I'm saying I'm glad I found her in there. I may be her only option for companionship right now, but I wouldn't be offended if she told me to get lost.

I'm not her knight in shining armour. I'm not going to be the one to save the day. I should keep my mouth shut, really.

Diana chuckles on the other side of the door. Her voice is

slightly muffled by the insulation of the door and fan of the cooling motor, but it still locks in my attention.

"I'm glad you've found me too," she says and I try not to let it go to my head. She's glad to be found. I don't need to be a part of this equation.

"Is there someone I should call to let them know you're safe?" I ask.

"Nope. No one," she says immediately before she adds, "Well that's not completely true. My brother will be worried if I don't call him after dinner, but he's used to not hearing from me all day when I'm working so as long as I'm not still in here this evening, I don't need to tell him."

At least I'm not some creepy guy sitting here with her while her actual boyfriend is at home assuming she's having a regular day at work.

"You don't have to wait here with me. I know the weather is bad outside, but I don't expect you to stay. You can help yourself to anything in the display case out front." My stomach grumbles just thinking about all the treats I saw when I walked in.

"I think I'll take a look," I say and then make my way to the café. I know Diana is right around the corner, but I feel bad putting any distance between us. I grab the first thing I see, a jar labelled 'energy bites.' They look like some sort of date and nut product that should hold my stomach over. I'm sure there are must tastier treats to be had but convenience outweighs taste right now. I don't want to risk having an upset stomach right now.

As soon as I'm back at the freezer door, I drop to sit on my butt with my back to the door. The thumping noise of my spine hitting the door must surprise Diana.

"You came back," she gasps, sounding relieved. Did she think I was just going to leave her there? I guess she doesn't really know me but there's no way I'm leaving until I know Diana is safely on my side of the door.

"I'm not going anywhere," I state, leaving no room for discussion.

"What do you want to do while we wait for help?" she asks, and I hate that I'm not able to help. If this was a computer, I would be all over it. I've been coding since I knew what it was and have made a living building software. I know nothing about the mechanics of anything in this building, aside from maybe the point-of-sale software.

"Tell me about yourself," I say. There's not much we can do besides talk so we might as well get to know each other.

"What do you want to know?" she asks.

"Anything," I say out loud. *Everything* I say to myself.

DIANA

"Um, Diana?" Henri asks, cutting me off mid-sentence. It's probably for the best. He doesn't need to hear about the disaster that was my high school prom. Who knew I had very few interesting stories about myself and many, many embarrassing ones?

"Yes?"

"Is there any reason it should be raining, inside?"

Rain? Inside? I'm about to respond when a drop of something very cold smacks me on the forehead. I look up and get another splatter of water right in my eye. *Ow.*

I pull away from the door and realize that my shirt wasn't just cold, from being pressed against the door, it's wet. The entire interior of the door looks like it's sweating.

"Diana?"

Shit, I almost forgot about Henri.

"Hey, Henri. Can you take a couple of steps away from the door?" I ask.

"Yes, sure." I hear him scuffle around and then he says, "Done."

I take a step toward the door, grab the handle and hold my breath while pushing the door open. A piece of melting ice falls from the door frame, shattering at my feet before the seal pops and warm air floods the space.

"Holy shit," Henri says and I look up to finally see his face. Shit, he's hot. His hair looks like it was once a rich dark brown, but it now has some flecks of grey throughout. He's tall and broad, filling out his sweater a little too well. And when his eyes meet mine, I have to hold the door frame for support. I don't think I've ever seen that colour of green so vibrant in someone's eyes before.

I'm just staring at him, and I know I should say something, but I'm speechless. I just spent the last hour telling *this* man, every embarrassing fact about myself. This is why I'm single. *This.*

I move my lips, to try and force words out. What words? No idea. But before my throat can form a sound, Henri has me locked in a warm embrace. I almost forgot that I was cold, but now with his arms around me, I feel like I'm snuggled up by the fire, with a mug of hot chocolate after a day spent in the snow. Or maybe it's hot apple cider considering Henri smells like he spends his spare time at an apple orchard.

And then Henri kisses me. ME. And it isn't a friendly peck on the cheek. It's all-consuming. I don't think I've ever felt this type of passion before, and although it wasn't the greeting I was expecting, I am not complaining.

His tongue fights its way into my mouth and I let it, meeting him stroke for stroke. He walks us backward until my back hits the far wall and I'm pinned against his body.

"Fuck, Diana," he mumbles between kisses. "Are you okay?"

I don't have the brain capacity to respond. My only thoughts are his hands all over my body, so I only nod in response.

"Shit," he says, pulling away. I hold in the whine that tries to escape. "You just went through something traumatic and I'm practically mauling you. I'm sorry."

"Don't apologize," I blurt out. "Maul me." *Maul me?*

I don't give either of us time to truly digest what I just said and instead, I loop my arms around his neck and jump so that my legs are wrapped around his waist. Maybe I did just go through something traumatic, but I don't really care. This sexy, kind man chose to sit on the floor and talk to me when he didn't owe me that. He could have called for help and then left. He could have robbed the place. But he didn't. He sat on the cold floor and shared stories about his life with me while I told him about mine. It may have only been a couple of hours, but it felt like months or years. Maybe I lost brain cells in the freezer, but I can't help but feel like Henri is meant to be someone special to me.

Henri chuckles. "Maul you?" he asks. Great, so he did hear me. His voice drops, "Is that what you want?"

I don't answer with words. I grind myself against the hard bulge under his jeans and nibble on his neck. "Fuck," he groans, and I feel my panties get even damper. "Are you sure?"

"Yes. Please."

"So polite," he coos. "Tell me what you want, Diana."

"You. I want you."

Henri squeezes my ass in his large hands, before moving them up to the hem of my sweater. He pulls it over my head before getting to work on my pants. I drop back down to my feet to help him get them off and then we both help him get out of his clothes.

He lifts me back into the air, pinning me against the cold wall, but the temperature doesn't bother me because Henri's thumb has found my clit and his fingers are working their way into me.

"Henri," I moan.

"Do you like that? Are you going to fuck yourself on my hand?" He asks while nibbling on my ear.

"I need more." I can feel his hard cock rubbing against my hip, so I know he wants more too.

"You want my cock?"

"Please," I practically beg. Is this what it's like to be with an older man? I'm a bumbling mess right now and he's hardly touched me.

Henri removes his hands from inside me. "Are you on birth control? I don't have a condom. My last test was negative." His words sober me for a moment. I'm about to have sex with someone who is practically a stranger but I've never felt so connected to another person before.

"I'm on the pill and I'm all clear. Please, Henri."

The words are barely out of my mouth before I feel him fill me completely. We're a mess of hands, lips, and teeth. I need all of him all over me. He takes my nipple into his mouth, kissing and biting. I run my fingers through his thick hair and pull hard. His hand drops between us, finding my clit. My nails rack down his back, hopefully leaving a mark.

He hits a spot deep inside of me and I scream out as an orgasm takes over. I hear him mumble, "fuck," before feeling his release inside me. He rubs his nose against mine and I can't help the big smile that takes up the majority of my face. I lean in for a kiss but freeze when I hear a loud shout, "BLUEFIELD FIRE DEPARTMENT." And then several heavy feet, running toward us.

HENRI

The entire Bluefield Fire Department is staring at my bare ass.

I wish this was a nightmare I could wake up from, but then the sex with Diana would have been a dream, and I don't ever want to wake up from that.

"Diana?" A voice behind us asks, and she hides her face in my neck. I'm thankful that my body is completely hiding her given that most of our clothing ended up scattered around the place. I look over my shoulder at a man in a Bluefield Police uniform. *Great, the police department gets to see my ass too.*

"I'm okay, Constable Peters," Diana mumbles without looking at anyone in the room. "The door opened, please all leave."

"It happened again?" he asks.

"Again?" I question. My mind immediately goes to Diana having sex in the freezer being a common occurrence but Diana's voice cuts through my train of thought.

"It was the fridge last time, thank you very much. And someone put a heavy box in front of the door. This time the door was frozen shut."

"You've been trapped before?" I ask quietly so only Diana can hear me.

"Yes," she says as her cheeks turn a cute shade of pink.

I don't know these people, but it seems like Diana does and I have to assume she doesn't want half of the first responders in town to see her in this position. I look over my shoulder and address Constable Peters. "Would you guys mind meeting us out front...Once we are better prepared to talk?"

Constable Peters at least has the good sense to look sheepish at the fact they are all standing there while we are mostly naked.

Constable Peters directs everyone out of the doorway to the freezer and out of sight. Once their voices sound far enough away, I slowly lower Diana to the floor and grab her discarded pants.

"That was mortifying," Diana whispers as she gets dressed.

"I'm sorry," is the only thing I can think to say, but it feels wrong. Based on the sad look in Diana's eyes, it was the wrong thing to say.

"If you are about to tell me you regret everything that happened between us, don't bother. Just leave," she says with fake confidence, her bottom lip trembles giving away the emotions she really feeling. I grab my sweater from the floor and slip it over her head to help her stay warm.

"I could never regret anything with you, Diana. I know we've only known each other for a couple of hours, but listening to your voice through the door was amazing. The second I saw your face I just knew I was meant to be the one to find you. Do you think we could continue getting to know each other?"

"Henri, you better not be friend zoning me right now."

"Only if that's how you want me. I'll be your friend, date you, love you, whatever you want, I'm in."

DIANA

"When Liana gets back from vacation, I'll talk to her about some upgrades she could do so that this doesn't happen again and if it does, maybe you store some warm clothes in there just in case. Now I'll let you guys get out of here before the next wave of the storm hits," Peters says after everyone else has left and he's taken our statements for his report. He leaves shortly after.

"No more getting locked into cold spaces, Diana," Henri mumbles against my hair. A shiver works its way down my body causing my nipples to harden and my toes to curl. I know he didn't mean for that to sound sexy, but the deep timber of his voice causes the dirty things he said against my ear in the freezer to play on a loop in my head.

"Good girl." "My cum is going to warm you up." "Fuck, baby, you feel so good."

"Diana," he grumbles. Clearly, my face is showing him exactly where my mind went.

"I promise to always give you the key," I say and Henri looks at me, confused. "The keys to my heart," I add. This is probably the cheesiest thing that has ever come out of my mouth but I don't care, because Henri pulls me into his warm hug and kisses the top of my head.

"I'll keep the key safe. Let's get you home," he says.

As we leave the café and I lock the door, Henri stays so close a part of him is always touching me. I get a whiff of the apple cinnamon again.

"Why do you smell like a fall candle?" I ask.

"I smell like what?" Henri looks horrified by the prospect. I guess my description doesn't give off masculine cologne vibes, but he smells like he lives inside a pie.

"You smell like apple," I correct.

"Oh. That. Yeah, there's an apple orchard outside of town that's for sale. My brother and I are looking for a new investment and with Dad living in town now, this made sense. I toured it yesterday. I guess the smell stuck to my coat."

"Oh my god! I have the best apple cream pie recipe. I'll have to make it for you sometime." My mind immediately filters through every apple-related recipe I know.

"I have a dairy allergy."

"But, but, butter is like my God."

"We'll figure it out," he states like it's that easy. But maybe it is with Henri. Because what should have been one of the worst days of my life so far, has ended with me walking down the winter wonderland streets of Bluefield. Henri's arm around my shoulder, mine around his waist and nothing has ever felt so right before in my life.

"We'll figure it out," I agree.

THE END

HEATHER GREY IS a Canadian author with a passion for romance—and just the right touch of suspense. After years spent in the financial world, she traded in spreadsheets for storylines and now crafts tales that weave love, drama, and a little mystery into every page.

When she's not writing or dreaming up her next plot twist, you'll find her curled up with a book, surrounded by her beloved pets, enjoying time with friends, or exploring the outdoors with family.

THE PATRON SAINT OF FUN SINGLES PACT WEEKEND

MADELINE NIXON

Tropes:

- Contemporary romance
- Enemies to lovers
- Forced proximity (snowed in)

Content Warnings: explicit sexual content (making out, handjob), death of a parent mentioned.

As I sit in my Toyota Prius that is woefully unequipped for blizzard weather, I rethink all my life choices. It's a miracle I wound up at my best friend Megan's family cottage alive. The highway? Totally fine. But the backroads of Prince Edward County were not meant to be travelled in this kind of snow.

And I am an absolute idiot for thinking anyone would uphold the Fun Singles Pact and show up here for Valentine's Day.

Megan's cottage is completely dark. There are no cars on the road and none in the driveway. I can't even make out where the driveway would be. There's about three feet of snow blocking my tiny car from pulling in anywhere.

So, this is how I die.

A totally ideal situation I've always pictured for myself.

Something in the back of my mind tells me I'll be fine. I've weaseled my way out of stickier travel situations. I got food poisoning at my cousin's destination wedding and still managed to make my flight home two days later. I did not get rabies from the cat that bit me in Punta Cana. Hell, I even survived a ferry sinking on my way to Mykonos.

A little (okay, a lot of) snow? This is not how I die. Absolutely no dying tonight.

A fist pounds against the window of my car and I shriek loud enough that it echoes in the small space. There might be a tiny chance that the random man whose hat is down so low and scarf is up so high that I cannot see any of his features will be my demise. But at least that's a better headline than *Stupid Influencer Dies In Blizzard*.

When the stranger outside my car is met with nothing but wide eyes and frantic scrambling to ensure that my doors are, in fact, locked, the knocking stops. Only to be replaced with a dramatic sigh and vigorous clearing of my water droplet-covered window.

"Dorothy, come on," the man of mystery says.

I freeze and squint at the two inches of skin I can see on this man's face. In the glow of my headlights, his eyes seem grey, framed by feathery eyebrows, and golden lashes. I wish I didn't know who he was from this little clue, but I do.

Are you kidding me???

Not only am I going to freeze to death. I'm going to freeze to death with Gus Adams.

With a sigh, I unlock the car and he slides his long body into the backseat. Unfortunately for him, I'm only five days back from an all-expense paid trip to New Zealand and the backbench is positively littered with freebies I haven't had time to go through. It's a wonder my car hasn't been broken into. He squeezes himself next to my suitcase filled with unidentified crap. I turn in my seat and watch him tug down his red scarf and huff in gulping breaths of air.

"Jesus, how much shit did you pack for a weekend?" Gus asks.

"Enough for the both of us, I guess. I see you've brought a grand total of nothing."

He snorts. "Bags are in my truck. Wasn't going to lug them over here in case you didn't let me in."

Okay, that's totally fair. He's only in my car right now out of pity. He genuinely looked like hypothermia was minutes away. Which does not make me feel great about whatever we have to do next.

"Why'd you come over then?"

"I was hoping you had a key."

Oh, of course. He didn't come over to check up on me. He came over to ensure his own well-being. I sigh and pull the black lanyard dangling every key I own from the cupholder. Gus's eyebrows shoot up, a smirk tugging at his lips, deepening two prominent smile lines.

"Much as I love a good game, are we really about to sort through a hundred keys in a blizzard? Your car is going to run out of gas by then, leading to almost certain death."

I roll my eyes and find the key Megan and I painted pink with glitter nail polish when we were twelve. Eighteen years later, it's chipped and sticks in the lock, but at least it's still easily identifiable.

"That key is a tragedy," Gus says.

I hold back from replying with something deeply immature, namely that Gus, himself, is a tragedy. It takes effort, a forceful swallow and dramatic exhale. I reach across the centre console for my hat and shove it overtop my dark staticky hair. The fuzzball on top brushes against the ceiling and I ignore the *ridiculous* grumble I hear from the backseat.

"Do you happen to have a shovel in your car?" I ask.

"Do you think I'm a murderer?"

"Obviously not, or I wouldn't have let you into my car or be entertaining the idea of spending, at least, one night in a cliché bumfuck nowhere lake house with you. I ask because you're always talking about how you're always doing other people's jobs. Is it not within the realm of possibility that you would have a shovel?"

"I presume nothing is really out of the realm of possibility… but there is no reason that anyone on set would ask me, the cameraman, for a shovel."

I rub my fingers against my brow bone as my eyes close. "Okay, so what do you suggest? Wade through three feet of snow until we reach the door?"

"I think that's maybe two feet, at best. But do you have a better idea?"

"What kind of bag did you bring?"

It takes us twenty minutes to wind up the needlessly long driveway to the front porch. My hardshell BÉIS suitcase leads the way, shoving snow to the side as Gus uses it as a makeshift snowblower, his own duffle bag slung over his shoulder. I snap a secret photo on my phone. Maybe I can make a travel nightmare post once we're *out* of this nightmare.

Gus collapses onto the sopping wet wicker bench next to the vibrant yellow wooden door. And I don't blame him. He took one for the team, albeit, without fully consulting me. I do blame myself for finding him attractive like this, though. I mean, panting and sweaty, kind of does something to a girl. I cringe away from the apparently unfrozen horny gremlin in my brain and pivot back to the door.

Please open.

With a click, the old lock turns. My key thankfully does not break. I nudge the door open with my foot, grab my suitcase, and slide into the darkened cottage. I feel along the wall until I find a light switch. But when flicked, nothing happens. For good measure, I flick it up and down approximately one hundred times. Still nothing. I groan, which twins with Gus's as he pushes himself off the bench and stumbles directly into me, his hand somehow landing on my ass.

"Hey!" I cry.

"Sorry!" he says, stepping back nearly onto the porch. "For the record, that was an accident. Most people don't stop right in the doorway."

I run a hand over my forehead. This is going to be a long night.

"We have no power."

"What?"

I flip on my cell phone's flashlight, illuminating the switch on the wall. "The power is out."

"So, naturally, standing by the door lamenting this fact is the way to go." Gus kicks the door shut and pulls his phone from his back pocket in one fluid motion, which shouldn't be hot because it's so mundane, but somehow is. Lord help me. "You know this place better than I do, I assume. I've been here once, you've been here—" he makes a motion with his hand, waiting for some indeterminate number "—many times. Do they have candles or flashlights somewhere?"

I should know this. At one point, I *did* know this. But I've been so busy the last few years that I can't remember the last time I was here. I haven't even seen my best friend since Christmas. I cut my trip short to be here and celebrate being alone together with Megan (and four of her closest friends). But I guess we know how that worked out.

I unlock my phone and find the Fun Singles Pact group chat. It's completely silent, save for a few weather-related messages this morning. It was barely snowing in Toronto when I left. Three hours sure changes a lot. I switch to my chat with Megan, one where her last text was detailing how excited she was to bake cookies, play games, and get drunk with me. I eye the darkened doorway to the kitchen. I know she stocked up in preparation and I'm pretty sure I need the wine if I'm going to survive the night with Gus.

DOROTHY: Hey girl!! Where tf are you??

MEG: ???? I'm at home?? Why where are you?

I send her a photo of the entryway, Gus hunting through the largely decorative credenza across from the front door. He jumps as the flash goes off, then shoots me a withering glare. I smirk and give him a three-fingered wave.

MEG: Omg!! Why are you there?? And is that Gus??

DOROTHY: We planned to be here! Why aren't YOU here?

MEG: I called it off earlier today!! We're literally in the middle of a blizzard. How did you even get there and not die??

DOROTHY: First of all, where did you do that?? And second, I genuinely don't know how I'm alive. Talk to me tomorrow, though. Gus and I might kill each other.

DOROTHY: Also, do you have candles?

Megan sends back the elusive candle location and apologizes

profusely. Because she did, in fact, call off the Fun Singles Pact Weekend today. She texted everyone except for me and Gus.

Fuck my life.

"Did you know there's a fireplace?" Gus calls from the den. A massive stone fireplace takes up an entire wall of the room, so yes, I did know this cottage had a fireplace. "And wood! There's a sizeable amount of wood!"

"Do you hear yourself?" I say, mostly to myself, but because the house is so empty, he hears me. And I only know that from the amused snort that echoes throughout the open concept of the first floor.

"Fear not, dear Dorothy!" Gus says, popping his head around the corner. "You needn't worry about wood with me. There are far too many beds in this house."

"Did you just make an only one bed joke?" I ask, incredulously. "How do you even know about that?"

He scoffs. "Dude, I work in TV. I grew up on TV Tropes. Only one bed is, like, the oldest trope in the book. Too many beds, though, that's peak comedy."

I roll my eyes and kick off my boots and soaking socks. Once inside the walk-in pantry of the professional-grade kitchen, I find a cabinet with a drawer two down from the top that holds any kind of candle you could desire. Tealights, birthday candles, votive, pillar, and one that looks a touch more phallic than your average wax pour. I pile candles out of the pantry and onto the marble countertop. And then, because curiosity killed the cat, I take out what is actually a candle shaped like a dick.

A massive dick.

I stand in place, and maybe in shock, and stare at the appendage for an unholy amount of time. My mind had somehow registered *a tip* within that drawer, but I didn't think it was a penis shaped candle, and a large one at that. But why would it even be here and what was Megan's plan with it?

I huff, blowing my slightly too long bangs out of my face, and exit the pantry one final time. I slam the cock candle down on the counter, accidentally cracking the outrageous balls. The laugh I've been holding back bubbles up my throat. My hands shake from the giggles as I snap a photo, more for the nightmare travel vault, then move to text Megan about my X-rated find. I have to know if she had some weird ritualistic wiener burning planned for Valentine's Day.

But I don't quite get that far.

Gus, smelling like a smoky forest and outfitted in a half-zip sweater that I kind of want to drown in, smirks just behind me. He bites his bottom lip before covering his mouth entirely and letting out a deep chuckle that rattles through him. He doubles over, though I'm not sure if it's from laughter or not wanting to look this thing directly in the eye.

"Gus," I say, but barely manage to get it out through my own sputtering laughs. "Gus! It's impolite to laugh at someone's size."

"Fuck off," he gasps and rights himself. "Here I thought I wouldn't have to worry about you with wood."

I groan at the terrible joke. "So, do we burn it?"

"I've waited all my life for someone to ask me that question."

I hand him the candle cock, then gather the tealights. Gus closes his eyes, trying to hold himself together, but his shoulders shake with the effort of silent laughter. Only then do I realize just how obscene this candle is. It was one thing for me to hold it and decide it's above average. It's another to see it in Gus's veiny man hands.

I shield my face from him, unsuccessfully keeping in my own laughter, and head into the den. The room is illuminated in the glow of the fireplace, which has also miraculously warmed up this corner of the house. I drop my wealth of candles onto the coffee table, then shed out of my puffy knee-length winter coat.

"You look like a burnt marshmallow in that coat," Gus says, plopping the candle of honour down in the centre of the table with a flourish.

I don't have a comeback for that, mainly because of the way his suede jacket fit him in all the right ways. So I roll my eyes while rearranging the candles so we have enough light, but don't burn down the house. Gus takes a few back to the kitchen and lights them on the counter. I straighten and watch as he gives me the greatest gift he possibly could, given our situation. He pulls wine and cheese from the depths of the fridge.

"Oh, thank God," I say.

"I am really doing the bare minimum here," he says. And maybe that's true since he didn't actually provide the food or wine. "But I appreciate the sentiment, no less. I'll be your God if you want."

My nose wrinkles as a combo cringe-groan overtakes me. "That may work in one of your TV shows, but not on me."

He lets out a snicker. "I really don't think that would work on TV, either. I just knew it would annoy you."

"Oh, great," I say and flop back against an anchor printed cushion. "Give me the wine, then."

The bottle of Pinot grigio drops onto the couch. I swipe it like the gremlin I am and eagerly open the screw top, which, obviously isn't as fun as a cork, but I'm all for ease right now. I tip the bottle to my lips and delight in the dry, slightly lemony taste. Gus places the cheese board between us on the couch, grabs the bottle from me, and takes a generous swig. He passes it back like it's contraband. I'm instantly transported back to high school, when Megan and I would secretly drink bottles she swiped from her parents' liquor cabinet while sitting at the top of the twisty slide.

I blink away the memory and take another long sip. This time, the taste bites its way down my throat. Gus's eyebrows raise as he reaches for a piece of cubed mozzarella.

"This feels like the antithesis to the Fun Singles Pact," I say.

"What, you think wine and cheese in front of a roaring fire is romantic?"

"Are you trying to seduce me?"

Gus laughs so hard, he snorts. And I'm not gonna lie, that kind of hurts. He shakes his head and swallows hard.

"Sorry, no," he says, then bunches his sleeves up to his elbows.

Ah, peak seduction. "I was just joking. I know you wouldn't be into that so I'm not trying to do anything." He glances at the wine and cheese, before his grey-blue eyes shift to the fire. "Though, I see how it looks."

I reach for a slice of Havarti and chew it while staring directly into the hearth.

"How did you start that?" I ask.

"What?"

"The fire. I mean, I get the action. I can start a fire. But did you caveman it or do you have a secret lighter somewhere?"

"Well, according to you, I'm a Boy Scout."

"When did I ever say that?"

Gus looks, quite possibly, the most amused he has ever looked. His eyes are positively gleaming, though it may just be the fire, and his lips are upturned so far that I swear he's going to sprout some green hair at the top of his head and turn into the Grinch. He's delighted in annoying me since the first time we hung out, a few days after Megan started a film elective and met him during her second year at what was then Ryerson University.

"You asked me for a shovel in your car and implied that I'm crafty. I'm a Boy Scout."

I narrow my eyes. "Were you ever actually a Boy Scout?"

"Fuck no, I hate camping. This cabin in the woods is as outdoorsy as I get. I founded the film club at my school. And I gotta tell ya, all that film knowledge has me half convinced some-one, or some*thing,* is going to jump out of that lake and right through those windows."

"You were such a nerd," I say, but my head slowly drifts toward the wall made up of entirely windows. It's pitch black out there. If I didn't know we were on a lake, I would think I was staring into an abyss. A shiver runs through me and I reach for the wine. "Secret lighter, then?"

He pulls a silver engraved lighter from his pocket and flips it open. The flame dances between us, before it abruptly goes out and our eyes lock.

"So are we going to ceremonially light the giant schlong, or what?"

I cackle, then throw my head back as I waterfall a stream of wine into my mouth. Gus takes the next gulp, apparently a necessary part of our ritual.

"All hail the big, beautiful penis. May our sacrifice bring forth what we truly desire," Gus says dramatically before lighting the tip and a few other tealights.

"Now what?" I ask.

"Now you bask in the glow."

"Sounds boring."

"I think I saw Scrabble over there."

I let out a pronounced sigh. "I'm so bad at Scrabble."

"Oh, Dorothy, my little ambiguous witch," he says and I scoff at the reference. "You have clearly not seen me play."

Gus jumps off the couch and saunters over to the fireplace. Beside it is a shelf stocked with beachy trinkets, a letterboard reading the Wi-Fi password we can't use sans-power, a collection of old and yellowed books, and a small stack of games. He pulls an old, battered version of Scrabble from the bottom. I bite my lip to hold back a laugh as he blows dust from the lid, as if he's unearthed a hidden relic like from the *Jumanji* movies.

I sigh and grab a handful of cheese before moving the board onto the floor. I desperately hope there's no secret critters living in the cottage, seeing as I still intend to eat the rest of this.

"Hey!" I say as Gus rejoins me and begins setting up the game. "Were there any crackers with this cheese? Maybe some meat or grapes?

"Sorry, it was just cheese. Did Megan come and get the house ready at some point?"

I shrug. "It's possible. She likes making sure everything's perfect."

"True. Are you ready for the worst game of Scrabble you will ever play?" Gus asks.

There's something endearing and boyish about his face in this light. Maybe it's the wayward curl falling onto his forehead, glinting golden at just the right angle. Whatever it is, it makes me want to trust him. To try and be nice. A corner of my lips lift, but I stuff my handful of cheese into my mouth before I can sabotage myself.

He snickers and pulls letter tiles out of the bag. "Okay, I'll go first."

I swallow my gob of cheese and reach for the wine. I slosh some out into my mouth, then reach for the letter bag. Gus and I swap items. He downs some wine like a shot and I place seven letters on my rack.

"I think I could win this tonight," Gus says, confidently laying out a six-letter word.

I squint down at the board, which we've unintentionally placed on the worst lit spot of the couch.

"Blonde?" I say and scoff. "You would."

His blond brow furrows. "What? What does that mean?"

"I don't know. It just feels kind of self-centred. Like, you are blond. And everyone knows that you shouldn't date guys with blond hair 'cause they're untrustworthy jerks."

"What, is that a rule?"

"More of an unspoken code." I rearrange my letters, trying to figure out a semi-decent word. Gus, on the other hand, is trying to hold back a laugh. "Same as how guys with J names tend to be awful." I pause and meet his eyes, dancing with amusement in the firelight. "You're only a few letters off and G can make the same sound so..."

"I'll have you know, my name is August."

"Are you a Taylor Swift song?"

He starts singing in an oddly high-pitched voice about wine and affairs. And though I am usually largely unfazed by this man's idiotic antics, I find myself laughing. I shakily put my tiles down, joining up with his O.

"Seriously, Dorothy?"

"I told you I was bad at this game!" I say.

"Right. Right. But 'come'? Were you inspired by the waxen output of the candle cock?"

My face crumples as I try to hold back what I know will be a very unattractive laugh. But my eyes slide over to our ritual sacrifice candle and find it positively dripping with wax. Vaguely ivory coloured wax, which is confusing, though perfectly on brand, considering the candle is bright pink.

I turn back to the board when I hear the tinkering of tiles. Gus's next word has joined with his first. Boobs.

"Are you shitting me?" I say.

"I am not shitting you," he says, completely deadpan. "I couldn't pass up the opportunity."

"Those are the only boobs you'll be getting this weekend," I say, adding a B and R to the E at the end of blonde.

"Now, don't tempt me, dear Dorothy." He hovers over the board. "'Breast'?? You call me out for 'boobs' and then copy my word?"

"I'm sorry. I didn't know you owned all the tits in the world." His lip quirks as he reaches for his letters. "Please don't tell me your next word is tit."

"No, but close."

Gus adds 'bluejay' to 'breast'.

"Nuh-uh," I say and flick one of his letters. "That's two words. You can't do that."

"You're only saying that because you're losing."

"I am not. I may not be good at this game, but I'm a stickler for the rules. You cannot play two words as one."

"Dorothy, it's literally just the two of us playing. Does it really matter?"

"Yes."

"*Really*? This is the hill you want to die on?"

"Yes."

"Fine," he says and his eyes flash. He picks up his tiles and returns them to his rack. "This is so you."

"What does that mean?"

His head snaps up. The fire I've watched dance in his eyes over the last half hour has shifted from playful into simmering anger. I've pushed one button too far.

"You're always so uptight. You never care about what anyone else has to say. It's your way or fuck off."

"All this over one word?"

"No, all this because you hate me for no reason and have since we were nineteen. I don't know what I did to you. You're holding this grudge and for what? What does it bring you?"

A pit forms in my stomach. We've thrown barbs for years without thinking. It always felt mutual, like we were both having fun while also being totally and completely annoyed by the very presence of the other person.

I glance down at my wrist and play with my mom's gold bangle I wear every day. I take a deep breath, not sure what I'm about to say. Whether it's an apology or fight...

Yeah, you know what, I'm not finished.

"Why do you think I didn't like you all those years ago? I didn't just look at you and decide you were the worst human I'd ever met." He lets out a deranged little snort. "Despite what I would have you believe about blond men...I didn't write you off until you opened your mouth. Megan said we'd get along and I believed her. But I have never heard you talk about anything other than yourself. Maybe I'm a stick-in-the-mud and like doing things right, but you are worse. You think you're so cool and so impor-tant. It's always *I have to fly out to this obscure filming location. Oh, you have this cool story? Well I worked on Locke & Key and met Stephen King's son. Guess what? My TV show just won!* Everything has to be about you and how great you are."

Gus stares at me, breathing even. A line creases between his eyebrows and his mouth opens and closes.

"Dorothy, I—" he sighs and shakes his head. "It's not worth it. Whatever. You're a travel influencer riding the coattails of *The Wizard of Oz*. Why do I care what you think of me?"

"Is that supposed to be a dig?"

"No, it's just weird that you're ribbing me for loving film, you know, *my job*, when your whole life is based around some old movie. It just seems kind of juvenile."

I can't control how my face falls when he says it. I've read hundreds, if not thousands, of hate comments on my blog and socials for *Follow Your Yellow Brick Road*. I delete them. Let them roll right off my back. But somehow, this hurts. I run my hand along the tattoo on my foot. *There's no place like home.* God, I wish I was home right now.

"Sorry, I overstepped." Gus eyes the line of text along my instep. "It means something to you. I get that. I'm sorry. I just—You have always been like this with me. We were teenagers when we first met. I was trying to impress you by talking about something I loved. You shot me down."

The air leaves my lungs. I remember meeting him one October at Fran's, a diner near their campus. I was lost, just quit school, and holding onto my budding travel blogger idea like it was a lifeline. Because it was. My vision was clouded by something the exact opposite of rose-coloured and seeing someone so bright and excited hurt me deeper than I expected. I lashed out at him and he, rightfully, shot right back. One stupid decision informed by a haze of grief spawned eleven years of... this.

"The summer before we met, my mom died," I say. The admission sits in the air between us, fire crackling the only sound. "Her favourite movie was *The Wizard of Oz*."

"Oh, Dorothy, I'm so sorry."

He reaches out, gathering my hands into his overtop of our losing game. I blink away the tears at the tenderness of the gesture.

"You were so happy," I say and shake my head. "And I know now that's no excuse. I don't think I realized I started this until right now. I was just so lost and upset and I'd ruined everything I'd worked for while you and Megan were right on track."

"I had no idea. I wouldn't have been so cavalier if I'd known."

"I wouldn't have wanted anyone to treat me differently, least of all some guy I just met."

He chuckles. "Some guy, eh?"

"There he is," I say with a watery smirk.

"And how are you doing now? Still lost?"

My first instinct is to hide behind my hair, something I haven't done in years. I haven't been this vulnerable in...forever. Work keeps me hopping from place to place, no time for connections beyond a night here and there. But the way he's looking at me now, the openness in his eyes that has always been there under our ugliness, makes me want to drop all my barbed wire and fences. I find myself drawing closer to him.

"I think I'm finding my way home," I say, bridging the gap between us.

His lips draw to mine like a magnet. The Scrabble tiles clatter onto the hardwood floor as I throw myself into his lap. I've had some standout, sparks flying kisses in my life, but nothing has ever felt as sensational as this. Our bodies collide, knowing that we've been fighting for a decade and finally get this sweet, glorious, stupid relief. Nothing has ever felt so right.

I hold his face to mine like I'm afraid I'll pull back and this will all be a dream. But his hands trail down my body, creep along my hips and stall on the curve of my ass making me all too aware that this is real. And I need more. I need to make up for lost time. I could have been kissing him for eleven fucking years. I drop my hands to his chest, then lower, working my way under his sweater. He gasps into my mouth and my whole body tingles. *I could have heard him make that noise for all those years.*

In our frenzied movements, I don't know who takes off his shirt, but suddenly it's on the ground and I'm faced with a surprisingly sculpted chest. My eyes roam his body and stutter on a tattoo along his collarbone,

"Lights, camera, action," I whisper. I ghost my lips on each of the three icons, then kiss up his neck until our lips are just centimetres apart. "You're such a nerd."

"I'm your nerd," he hisses, then pins me down onto the couch.

If this is nerdy behaviour, then I'm all in. He rips open my blouse and I don't even care that a few buttons pop off because that was fucking hot. I shift, throwing the shirt away and undoing my bra simultaneously. His eyes darken as his pupils expand, greedily drinking me in. I grin, unabashed, as I see what I've done to him. His pants tent as he strains to be let out. And taking pity on him, I do exactly that. I reach for his belt, slip it off, then slide my hand down. Everything in me coils into a ball at the moan I elicit from him as I wrap a hand around his shaft.

"Do you have a condom?" I ask.

He groans, low and guttural, which does something to my already fluttery insides. "No. I wasn't expecting—"

"Right. Fun Singles Pact. We could look...later. We can do other things now," I say while running my closed fist up and down the length of him.

"Other things," he murmurs, cupping a large hand against the swell of my breast.

I laugh. "I guess I was wrong. You are getting tits tonight."

"Thank God," he says and leans down to kiss me.

However, he does not reach me because a cold shower comes in the form of my phone loudly ringing. We freeze. Stare at it. Let the ringtone die. Then exhale.

Until it rings again.

I groan and reach for the phone, Megan's name appearing on the screen. Gus's phone buzzes against the coffee table next.

"What the fuck?" he mutters.

We pick up our respective cells and answer them on the couch, half-naked and horny.

"Hello?"

"Dorothy! You're not going to believe this, but I think I'm in love!"

"I'm sorry...You're in love?" I question and, weirdly enough, Gus says something very similar to his mystery caller.

"The power went out at my condo and I got trapped in the elevator with that hot guy who lives on the floor below me. Anyway, power's back on and I'm at his place. He's dreamy. We literally just talked about nothing and everything for an hour. Can you believe it??"

"And on Fun Singles Pact Weekend!"

She giggles. "I know. I guess it was meant to be."

I end my call at the same moment Gus does. He stares at me with a half-smile, eyes wide and bewildered. His buddy Chris, who was also coming to Fun Singles Pact Weekend, has fallen in love. He caught a woman on the sidewalk just before she face-planted into a snowbank. Everything fell into place and bam. Love.

I shake my head in disbelief. Did the final member of our troop also find love today? Did we? Gus's hand finds my cheek, his thumb absently drawing circles. My eyelids flutter shut as he places a kiss on my forehead.

"Do you think it was the candle cock?" he whispers.

I crack up. The candle is positively dripping wax now.

"All hail the candle cock, patron saint of Fun Singles Pact Weekend." I kiss Gus as he chuckles. "And I couldn't be happier."

THE END

MADELINE NIXON HAS BEEN a dog walker, a nanny, a baker, a chocolatier, and an editor, but the title she's most fond of is author. She's published ghost stories, several educational children's books, and the romance series *Like A Love Song*. Her most recent release was a brother's best friend romance, *Not Actually*. When she's not writing, you can find her hunting ghosts, planning elaborate theme parties, and baking new recipes. She lives in a suburb outside of Toronto. You can learn more about her via her website, www.madelinenixon.com/.

THANK YOU

Thanks so much for picking up *Heart's Lock, Love's Key!* If you enjoyed the stories within, we would appreciate a quick review on the book retailer of your choice.